CADEYRN

Immortal Highlander, Clan Skaraven Book 2

HAZEL HUNTER

HH ONLINE

Hazel loves hearing from readers!
You can contact her at the links below.

Website: hazelhunter.com

Facebook:
business.facebook.com/HazelHunterAuthor

Newsletter: HazelHunter.com/news

I send newsletters with details on new releases,
special offers, and other bits of news related to
my writing. You can sign up here!

Chapter One

W EDGED IN A corner beside a
wooden bin, Lily Stover
listened to the winter wind
wailing outside the granary. Silly as it seemed,
she wished she knew what time and day it was.
Her watch had been smashed during her last
beating, and calendars probably hadn't yet
been invented in fourteenth-century Scotland.
She'd tried keeping count in her head, but the
rotten weather and her own exhaustion
blurred one day into the next. They might
have been here a week, a fortnight, or even
a month.

It felt like forever.

At least the bitterly cold gusts couldn't get
at her in her new medieval prison. The

storage building's thick stone walls had no windows, and something heavy barred the only door from the outside. For that she should be grateful, as she had only the torn, dirty clothes on her back and her sodding safety shoes, which had started to come apart at the seams.

As long as her mind didn't do the same she'd be aces.

Staying alive didn't make her heart glow with gratitude. Since being taken from her time she'd been subjected to malicious beatings, beastly conditions, and constant starvation. Her entire body felt like one great minging bruise. Working double shifts as a sous-chef in the *Atlantia Princess's* busy, cramped galley had never left her feeling this filthy or knackered. If by some staggering stroke of luck she ever made it back to the twenty-first century, she was never again stepping one foot off that bloody cruise ship.

"Can we eat grain, Lily?"

She looked up at Emeline, the black-haired Scottish nurse who had been taken with her and the two Thomas sisters. Throughout their ordeal she'd looked after everyone without complaint, even ignoring her own wrenched shoulder and badly-bruised jaw to tend to their injuries.

Her question perplexed Lily. They had no food other than the stingy rations the guards tossed in once a day.

"What are you on about?" The hoarse sound of her own voice made her stomach surge, and she tried again. "Sorry. You've found something to eat?"

"Maybe." Emeline led her over to another bin at the back of the granary. She raised the heavy lid to scoop out a handful of grain. "I think it's wheat, but I'm not sure." She glanced over her shoulder at the sisters before she murmured, "Perrin hasn't been eating for days."

Perrin Thomas, the older of the sisters, sat on the floor staring at nothing. A professional dancer, she'd been slender from the start. She'd lost at least a stone since they'd been brought back in time, whittling her delicate features and long limbs to a skeletal gauntness.

"She'll do better," Lily said. She'd talked to her last night about that and several other things, and the dancer had promised to try to eat enough to keep up her strength. "Let's have a look at it."

Lily inspected the kernels, which had been winnowed to remove the indigestible hull. She sifted her fingers through it to look for rot or mold, and then popped a grain in her mouth to chew it. The nutty flavor confirmed what it was.

"It's barley, but it seems all right." She squinted at the nurse's swollen jaw. "Soaking it for an hour will make it softer."

Emeline gave her a lopsided smile. "No water yet."

No water. Not enough food. No blankets or medicines or bandages or help. The nurse always tagged her inventories of their depriva-tions with that optimistic word—*yet*—but she knew as well as Lily what they couldn't depend on: hope.

A pair of golden ducat eyes, burning like cognac flambé, glared at her from her memory. They belonged to the nameless Scot-tish warrior who had tried to rescue her at the mountain sheep farm. When Lily had been snatched out of his reach and carried off, he'd let out a roar of fury that still echoed in her head. He'd kept riding after her, up to the moment when the mad druids had forced them into the portal and brought them here.

He hadn't given up on her, and neither would she—not yet.

"Pound it with a stone first," Lily said. "That'll break up the kernels into smaller bits. Should be easier to swallow."

When Emeline nodded and went back to the sisters, Lily sank down beside the bin. She leaned her head back and closed her eyes. She knew she should try and eat, but reliving those precious few seconds she'd seen the man with the strange, glowing tattoo on his arm gave her the only comfort she'd known since being snatched from the outdoor market.

Other, uglier memories decided to come first.

The day before she'd been taken, Lily had received a vile letter from her father's solicitor, sternly informing her that she'd been disinherited. Gourmet restaurateur and food magazine publisher Edgar Stover had reluctantly revealed that she, Lily Elizabeth Stover, wasn't his biological child. Of course, as a bastard she had no claims to financial provision under

Britain's Inheritance Act of 1975. She was, unequivocally, cut off without a pound from the wealthiest epicure in the UK.

Through the rest of her shift Lily had smiled. When one of the pastry chefs had asked her what was so amusing, she'd laughed and said, "I'm penniless."

To celebrate after work, she'd taken a demi of champagne back to her cabin to drink. Then she'd been sick, but even chundering half the night had felt glorious. At last she'd been freed. Edgar would never have her dragged back to London now. The drinking binge and her almost-delirious happiness had made her reckless. The next morning she'd asked for shore leave for the first time in six months. The head chef had agreed, with the condition that she buy some local produce for him. She'd practically skipped down the gangway to the dock at Invergordon.

Lily opened her eyes, but she couldn't stop seeing the rest. Renting a scooter and riding out into the country had been such fun. She'd stopped at a small farmers market where she'd found the sweetest gooseberries she'd ever sampled. Then the earth had exploded around her, and a huge thing shaped like a cracked-faced plastic rugby player had grabbed her by the neck.

Her trembling hand went right to her throat, and she swallowed a mouthful of bile. Those unspeakable moments should have been blurry, but instead they'd been etched on her brain. The thing had dragged her like a carcass toward the hole in the ground. There'd been the sickening crack of bones, then the silent screaming inside her head when she'd realized what he had done to her. She'd watched as, with one blow, the thing had bashed in the head of an old farmer who had tried to save her. Then she'd been pulled underground, and through the ground, only to be hurled into another pit filled with thrashing branches. When she'd finally landed in the fourteenth century, somehow she'd staggered to her feet to run. The thing had caught her again, and tried to strangle her before another one pushed it away.

You cannae kill this one. The Wood Dream need all five.

The scraping, groaning sound outside the granary brought Lily to her feet. Emeline quickly hauled Perrin away from the door, while the dancer's younger sister, Rowan came to stand in front of it. The slushy ground outside slopped as footsteps approached, and then a thin, middle-aged man with silver-streaked dark hair and viper-green eyes stepped inside.

"Good morning, Sisters." Hendry Greum tucked his hands behind his back, making his voluminous robe sway as he surveyed them all. "I trust you're well?"

"With no blankets, food, or water?" Rowan snarled back at him. "What do you think?"

Emeline came to stand beside the carpenter, and touched her shoulder before she said to Hendry, "We're injured and exhausted, but with some proper food and rest we'll recover. If you continue the kind of abuse we suffered at the forest farm, I doubt any of us will survive another week."

The druid nodded. "Until last night I wasnae aware of how badly your conditions became. You shall be given the provisions and care you require, but first I'll need something in return."

Rowan tensed and leaned forward. "We don't have—"

"Quiet," Emeline snapped, silencing the carpenter as she pulled her back. She turned to Hendry. "What do you want?"

"One of you has a new talent." He scanned their faces like a hungry fox inside a full coop. "A talent used to help Althea Jarden during the Skaraven attack. It caused injury to many of our *caraidean*, and that I willnae have. Tell me who has the mind-move gift, and the three who didnae help our enemy shall be well-treated and kept safe."

Rowan made a rude sound. "Like we're going to fall for that. The minute you leave, the beatings and starvation will start all over again."

"I've no plans to leave," the druid told her. "But should I need to, I'll leave Ochd with orders to stand guard over you."

Perrin rose to her feet and walked up to Hendry. "So all we have to do is give you the collaborator, and the rest of us get to live? We'll really be safe?"

"You have my word on it," the druid said.

The dancer backed away from him, and

then turned around to point at Lily. "It was her. She's the one who can move things with her mind."

The betrayal froze everyone, until Rowan shattered the shocked silence with a horrified, "Perrin, no."

Lily made a dash for the door, but Hendry caught her easily and clamped an arm around her neck.

"My thanks, Sister," he told Perrin. "I'll send Ochd with provisions directly."

Lily knew trying to struggle out of the druid's hold would be impossible. Hendry was nearly as strong as the things that served him and his crazy bint. Still, she fought him as he dragged her out of the granary, and took one final look at Emeline and the sisters before Ochd closed the door and wedged a huge round stone slab against it.

"My *caraidean* require recompense for what you did to them," Hendry said as he marched her toward the forest behind the old mill. "I believe I'll give you to them. They'll want some sport before they end you."

For show Lily considered biting a chunk out of his arm, but then he might change his mind. Instead she waited until they were out of earshot of the other captives before she stopped resisting him.

"They'll need a wash and clean clothes along with the food and doctoring. You'll see to it?"

"Aye." As soon as a big wooden cart hid them from view Hendry released her and stepped back. "Only ken that if you dinnae return by sunset with the location of Dun Mor, I shall give the nurse to Coig for his amusement. Can you fathom what he may do to her?"

Coig, the most sadistic of the things, had been the one who had taken Lily from the market. She knew exactly what he was capable of.

"Find Althea and you'll find Dun Mor," Hendry said. "You ken what will happen if you journey back to your time?"

She swallowed hard past the painful constriction in her throat. How would she ever be able to forget? She eyed the forest trail that led to a small oak grove. The bargain she'd struck with the druid had been the only solution to save herself and the other women. She still wondered if she'd ever stop feeling as if slime covered her from head to toe.

"I'll see you later," Lily said and shifted her gaze to the cart.

She drew on the ever-smoldering outrage in her heart. Inside her head a painful, restricting pressure built until she hurled it at the cart. The weathered wheels creaked and shuddered before the cart lifted into the air. Soil and bits of chaff rained down as Hendry backed away. A moment later the cart overturned and crashed where he had stood.

Lily heard the shouts of the guards as she ran for the trail, ducking under low branches and dodging brush as she hurried to the grove. The slushy ground made every step she took slide, but she managed to keep herself upright until she reached the clearing.

Snowdrops punctuated the melting drifts, promising a spring that wouldn't come for months. Lily halted, dragging in air as she focused on the center of the grove, where a circle of old, small stones poked up through the frost-furred grass.

She trembled as she approached the edge and watched the ground fall away into a dark, whirling pit. Once more she pushed back the ugly temptation to use the portal to return to her own time. If she saved herself, she knew Hendry would take it out on the others before he came to the future to hunt her down—not that she'd be terribly hard to find, or have a hope of escaping again.

Lily closed her eyes, but she didn't think of Althea. The botanist couldn't help her. She needed him, the man with the owl tattoo.

Chapter Two

T ETHERING HIS MOUNT and
stepping out of the forest, Cadeyrn
Skaraven found his sword hilt with
his hand. The gathering of villagers selling
their crops seemed peaceful enough, but his
experience as a war master told him something here would soon go amiss. The air felt
too still, and all the birds had gone quiet.

His eyes shifted as he took in the cloth-
tented stalls and the strange garments the
people wore. When had females begun
wearing trews? The bright, unnatural colors
of their garments made him squint. What
drew those huge painted trunks on wheels
across the grass? He had yet to spot a single
horse. Why had none of the men armed

themselves? Had they not heard of the *famhairean* being freed of their not-so-eternal prison, and returning to wreak death and destruction on their world?

His owl battle spirit enabled him to see weakness in anything, but he couldn't fathom what his eyes told him. Had some brain rot crept into these folk, that they milled about like placid sheep when the world had become a slaughter pen?

"Naught thought, naught seen," Cadeyrn muttered under his breath.

A young woman in a white coat and dark trews stepped into the sunlight, smashing through the tangled worry of his thoughts. In his dreams Cadeyrn had seen her sleek mane of streaked gold too many times to count, and still it fascinated him. She wore the shining mass coiled in a simple twist at the back of her head, pinned there by a long silver clasp. The sun had painted roses on her sculpted cheeks and ambered her pretty skin, suggesting she spent much time in it. A dairy maid, then, or perhaps a shepherdess. Her eyes, bright and large, glinted like dark emeralds as she inspected the fruits for sale. She accepted some berries from a farmer, and her lashes fluttered with pleasure as she tasted them.

Cadeyrn felt her delight from across the hill as if she had kissed his mouth to share the sweetness.

The lady smiled as she gave an old farmer some folded paper in exchange for a basket of the berries. She offered her thanks in a low purr of a voice that stroked down Cadeyrn's spine. He had always wondered what would be revealed as his own weakness. Now he knew. Longing for a female had never plagued him. Finding release with a pleasure lass had always eased him, nothing more. But this fair lady made his blood burn with hunger. He wanted a dark room, a bed strewn with soft linens, and her naked with him.

Gods, he would give anything to have a night alone with that green-eyed temptress.

The ground shook under his feet as if his very thoughts had offended, but Cadeyrn sensed something far less sacred. He watched for the earth to rise, and when it did he ran for the lady. Soil blasted into the air as the giant erupted from the ground, his body bespelled to resemble a huge mortal. Shrieking villagers scattered as he seized the lady by the neck and dragged her back to his pit. When the old farmer jumped in front of him the *famhair* crushed his skull with one clout.

Cadeyrn saw his lady's beautiful eyes widen with horror just as he reached them, but when he used his blade the sword passed through the giant's neck as if the metal were smoke. As the giant dropped with the lady into the earth, Cadeyrn jumped in after them, and landed on cold, unyielding stone.

He lay there for a moment as the scent of green juniper filled his head. Opening one eye, he saw the lower half of his chamber at Dun Mor. Blood dripped from his lip as he pushed himself upright. He'd split it again falling on his face. The next time he bonded with the water, it would vanish. Such was one of the gifts of being awakened from his grave as an immortal.

"Facking dreams."

He wiped the blood from his chin and regarded it for a long moment before he went to wash. Perhaps this nightly idiocy was some torment he'd brought back from the afterlife— if there had been one. All Cadeyrn remembered was dying on the battlefield with his clan one moment, and then clawing his way out of the ground the next. According to the druids that had brought the Skaraven back to life, twelve centuries had passed between those two moments. Immortal or not, a man could drive himself mad contemplating such inconceivable events.

Madness might be the reason for his dreaming of Lily Stover, a lass he'd never met.

Seeing Lily taken from the forest farm was as close as Cadeyrn had gotten to her. As soon as she'd been grabbed he'd ridden like a berserker to reach her, only to see her vanish with the mad druids and their *famhairean* into an oak grove. By the time he'd leapt off his horse the portal in the center of the grove had closed over. He dimly remembered gouging holes in the indifferent ground with his pounding fists. He'd gone daft, as if Lily were his lady, and they had stolen her from him. In that moment he'd been convinced he'd never have another chance to save her. For in truth, the next time he saw her she would likely be another of the broken, mangled corpses the evil scunners left in their wake. His lady was as lost to him as was his place in his own time. Mayhap 'twas the reason she haunted him.

She's no' your lady, you addled conniver.

Jerking on his trews, tunic and boots, Cadeyrn sheathed a dagger and sword on his belt. As he made his way through the stronghold, his battle spirit allowed him to see what others could not. He'd never matched Brennus's fearless raven agility, Ruadri's blinding moon power or Kanyth's fiery strength. Even Taran, the clan's quiet, mild-tempered horse master, had always been invincible on a mount. But as war master, Cadeyrn's sharp eyes allowed him to see into the weakness of a thing.

Now he watched for a lass he couldn't see. What a fool he was.

Night sentries nodded to him as he left Dun Mor and endured a buffeting icy wind to make his way to the new stables. As one of the clan's masters he had the freedom to come and go as he wished, and tonight it pleased him to ride the perimeter. He felt a twinge of sour amusement as he found his gray stallion saddled and ready to ride.

"I've grown unsurprising, have I, Liath?"

he asked the horse, which dipped his head for a nose rub. "My thanks, Taran."

The horse master appeared outside the open stall door, his pale, braided hair tied back from his lean, enigmatic face. He tossed him a tartan made of black and evergreen plaid.

"Dinnae ride him all night," Taran said. "Unlike us, Liath craves his sleep."

Cadeyrn led the stallion out through the rocky enclosure that concealed the stables, and mounted him with fluid ease. He'd missed riding since being brought back from the grave, but with winter coming there would be fewer chances to roam. The coldest months in the *Am Monadh Ruadh* brought endless ice and snow storms. When the weather cleared in the Red Hills, the cold remained, often too icy to inflict on the mounts for long.

But there was no ride that would be long enough. Though it helped exhaust him, it never kept away the dreams of Lily.

Why the horse master had given him the tartan for his ride became clear. The first scouts of winter had crept into the ancient forest. Frost glistened everywhere around the Skaraven stronghold. The spiky ice furred the

leafy carpet beneath Liath's hooves to a
ghostly silver. Wood smoke from Dun Mor's
hearths wafted through a series of chambered
vents before dispersing through hundreds of
small flues spread beneath the great plateau.
Any intruder entering their territory might
smell their presence, but they'd never locate
them.

Their Chieftain, Brennus, had spoken of
using their power and experience to protect
the innocent, but Cadeyrn still wondered if
they'd ever truly be free. The Skaraven had
been bred as indentured warriors, enslaved to
fight for and defend the two Pritani tribes that
had created them. Hardship and battle had
always been their lot. They'd never been
permitted to live among the Pritani. Until
Brennus's mate, Althea Jarden, had come to
Dun Mor, none of the Skaraven had even
spoken to a female.

When the tribes had died of sickness, the
Skaraven had been freed for a short time, and
came to the Red Hills to build Dun Mor and
live as a clan. Now they had returned, but they
still had no claim on the Great Wood. Nearly
everything they'd owned in their mortal lives

had rotted away, and they'd been forced to accept necessary goods from the tree-knowers. Even the tartan Cadeyrn wore belonged to another clan.

"Someday soon we'll have our own," he told Liath.

Riding to the outer boundaries of the forest, Cadeyrn moved down the lower slopes and followed the river that had brought them home. Along with eternal life, the druids had given the clan the ability to bond with water, and use rivers, lochs and streams to travel great distances in but a few moments. The advantage it gave them would come only when they learned at last where the *faimhairean* had hidden away. The chieftain had been sending out search parties every day, but Caledonia was a very large country.

"Scotland," Cadeyrn muttered, correcting himself. "They call it Scotland now."

How long he'd ridden, Cadeyrn didn't know until the first rays of dawn illuminated the horizon. With a grimace, he once again turned Liath toward home. If the mad druids had decided to go into hiding, it might take them years to find them and the giants.

Thinking of his green-eyed lady in their care for so long made Cadeyrn's gut clench. He knew how brutal and unfeeling the giants were. The mad druids who led them had proven to be just as sadistic. Better he not think of Lily at all–

"Help me," a rasping voice called from the other side of the river.

As Cadeyrn dismounted, he drew his sword. But even as he peered across the water, something in his chest knotted. His battle spirit stirred and yet his eyes found no danger.

Could it be, that after all the searching–

A thin shape lurched behind the brush as a sliver of sun glinted on golden hair. With a muffled cry, he jumped into the water. Despite the river's strong, frigid currents, he hurtled across, leaving a wake behind him. But when he reached the opposite shore and bounded up the bank, he stopped. Still peering into the trees, every nerve was alight. Heart pounding, he forced himself to slowly sheath his sword before he stepped into a patch of daylight.

"My lady?" he called softly, almost afraid to hear her response.

To his disbelief, she stumbled out of the

woods, made directly for him, and flung herself into his arms. Instinctively he caught her, holding her shaking, slender body tight against him until she gripped his tartan and drew back. Lily Stover looked up at him, her chest heaving and her eyes filled with desperation and tears.

"Are you Skaraven?" she asked, rasping the words.

"Aye," Cadeyrn managed to say as her knees gave out and he caught her. He wrapped an arm around her waist, pushing aside his shock to reassure her. "Stay with me, lass. Dinnae try to speak just now. Catch your breath."

She pressed her brow to his shoulder, still quaking as she nodded, while Cadeyrn silently marveled. Lily Stover was real—and she was with him.

She stood tall for a female, but the top of her head fit neatly under his chin. Her body felt wand-thin, but over her long bones he could feel sleek muscle. Her heat sank through his tunic and spread over his chest, soft and saturating. He'd never known what other men felt when they held their sweethearts and wives. Now he understood why they lingered so long in such embraces. The fierce protectiveness that welled up in him brought with it a flicker of shame. To think he had once worried that Brennus might harm Althea if the chieftain were not chained… Gods, how thick-headed he'd been.

Lily murmured something, and he loosened his hold. "What did you say?"

"I can't believe you're here, that I found you." She lifted one hand to touch his cheek. "I saw you riding after me when they took us." Snatching back her fingers, she shook her head. "Sorry, I'm still a bit shambolic."

"'Twill be well now," he assured her.

Althea had told him that Lily came from England, which explained the differences in their accents, but not the hoarseness in her voice. Gently he brushed the tangled hair back from her bruised face, and saw more marks on her throat. No wonder she spoke as if every word hurt her, she'd nearly been strangled. Seeing the signs of her suffering ignited a deep, seething hatred in him.

"I'm Cadeyrn." She didn't need to hear that he was the clan's war master. The poor

lass would be terrified of him. "Or Cade, if
you like. How did you come here?"

"Right," she said, and took in a deep
breath. "They learned that I helped Althea
during the fight. When they marched me out
to kill me, I broke free and ran for the grove."

Cadeyrn saw the guilty way she averted
her gaze, and imagined she was thinking of
the three lasses she'd left behind.

"If you'd tried to free the others, you'd
never have escaped."

"Oh, I'd have made a hash of it. Still
could." She pressed her lips together and then
looked up at him. "Will you go back with me,
and help get them away?"

He'd like nothing better but he'd already
felt the shredded sleeves of her jacket, and the
warmth of blood soaking through it. She also
had dark stains and broken nails on
both hands.

"We'll speak to my chieftain, but first you
need tending." When her face fell he quickly
added, "Lady Althea awaits in the stronghold." Shock widened her eyes. "Aye. She'll
have much to tell you."

And Brennus needed to hear of a sacred

grove so near the stronghold. But as he moved to help her toward the water, she held up a hand.

"Wait," she said and showed him one of her feet, which was clad only in a wet stocking. "One of my shoes fell off when I came out here. Might we fetch it first?"

He felt tempted to carry her to the stronghold, and yet at the same time he longed to do this small thing for her. But as his war master senses returned, he knew it would also do well to inspect the portal.

"Let's see this grove then," he said, nodding.

As she led him back into the trees, Cadeyrn saw why they'd never discovered the place. As they approached, she slipped away from him to climb onto a high mound of stones. When he joined her he saw a second, inner ring made of scattered rocks around a patch of glowing ground. Behind the stone mound a crescent-shaped cluster of ancient oaks loomed, concealed from behind by a wall of thick-needled pines.

"I don't think I can reach it," she said,

pointing to a small black slipper near the edge of the portal. "Can you?"

Cadeyrn crouched, and leaned down to retrieve it, only to feel Lily leap past him. As he stood, she bent and touched the ground, which whirled out into an open portal. All the emotion left her pale face as she stood and stared at him.

"Lass, you cannae—"

Her eyes went black, and then a huge force slammed into the back of his head. Lily said something as the world went dark, and he fell into the spinning chasm.

Chapter Three

✦❦✦

ANCIENT FORESTS AS far as the eye could see surrounded Bhaltair Flen and Oriana Embry as they rode their ponies toward their unhappy destination. He'd told his acolyte that they would be riding through trees older than even druid kind, but Oriana seemed somewhat indifferent to their magnificence. Perhaps the prospect of visiting a place where so many had died occupied her thoughts. It certainly disturbed his own, along with other troubling signs.

Since entering the dead tribe's territory Bhaltair had felt the absence of other lives. He heard no birdsong, which added a peculiar emptiness to the still, dry air. Nor had a single forest creature appeared to look out at them.

The few trees that had not dropped their leaves in preparation for winter had a dullness to them, as if their evergreens had gone ashen.

Twelve centuries had passed since the Wood Dream tribe had been attacked and slaughtered by marauding Romans. Still the land mourned as if their blood had been spilled yesterday. Perhaps because the massacre had spawned the blood-thirsty *famhairean* it might never heal.

For many centuries Bhaltair had not permitted himself to think on the lost tribe. He could excuse himself for being preoccupied with other, equally dire matters, but the truth was that he had deliberately forgotten the Wood Dream and their terrible legacy. Of late he'd tried to make amends for that, particularly to the Skaraven Clan, who had long ago died while helping him entrap the *famhairean*. His gift of awakening the clan to immortality had not swayed their hatred of him an inch. Their chieftain, Brennus, had told him as much before taking his clan and disappearing. Perhaps nothing would repair the damage Bhaltair had done, but if he could find the means to defeat the giants, it would hold some weight with Brennus and his men.

"Master, 'tis been so long since the Wood Dream disincarnated," Oriana said, her timid voice low and hushed, as if she feared waking the dead. "Surely we willnae find anything of them here."

"Aye, time serves as the world's scrub maid. Yet it cannae wash away that which has no incarnation." He reined in his mount and peered ahead. "You see that ring there, between the two trenches that lead into the woods? 'Twas once a ritual altar."

Her soft eyes narrowed as she squinted at the spot. "Those jagged rocks poking through the moss? Surely no'."

"They arenae stone, but wood turned to it. The tribe used the stumps of fallen sacred oak to build their altars. 'Twas said that the Wood Dream even spoke to the trees." Slowly he dismounted and retrieved his cane from a saddle loop. "Come now, dear one. We shall walk from here."

Once Oriana had hobbled their mounts she retrieved their packs and brought him a flask of water. "You must drink, Master. I see the sweat glistening on your brow. 'Twill no' do for you to become parched."

"My thanks," Bhaltair said and took a few swallows before mopping his face with a kerchief. "I cannae, for the lives of me, ken why I grow so hot in such chill weather."

"I dinnae think you're heated." Her face grew solemn as she regarded the old altar. "I almost feel them here. When the tribe died beneath Roman blades, the violence sank with their blood into the earth. Our poor brothers and sisters, how they must have suffered. Like my grandfather at the hands of the *famhairean*."

He saw how she shuddered. "Dinnae think on it, Oriana."

"Naught else fills my head," she said with grim conviction before she grimaced. "Forgive me, Master. My prattling delays us."

"Nonsense. I'm your teacher. If you cannae speak your mind, you maynae learn." He took a better grip on his cane, and used it to point to the long stretch of barren, stony soil. "See, there now. The tribe used the old way of pebbling their trails to preserve them. I reckon that one shall lead us to their settlement."

They followed the rough ground into a thicket of birch and pine, where the air grew latticed with thin shadows from the skeletal canopy overhead. Now and then Bhaltair spotted heaps of smooth stones scattered over roots, and imagined them to be the remains of spell cairns placed to ward off mortal intruders. They had continued to do their work even after the tribe's demise. From the thickness of the leaf and twig rot, no one had used the path in centuries.

"'Tis so quiet and empty here," Oriana murmured. "If someone died in these woods, I reckon no one would ever come upon them."

"Well, then, dinnae kill me here," Bhaltair said. "For I wish a proper burial." He saw the stricken look in her eyes. "I but jest with you, dear one. I trust you with my life."

She nodded quickly. "I shall try to be worthy of that, Master."

The trees thinned and then parted around them as they reached a clearing large enough to accommodate a modest village. The Wood

Dream's cottages and outbuildings had long ago fallen and rotted away, leaving only a few stone hearths, now toppled or crumbling beneath grim blankets of dead vines. Golden mistletoe grew unchecked everywhere, decking the trees in magic splendor. At least the sacred vine proved that druids had once occupied the place, but Bhaltair saw no other trace of the lost tribe.

Oriana stopped and turned slowly. "'Tis all gone." She met his gaze. "I cannae feel anything here but shadows and ruin."

"We ken 'twould be a gamble, lass. 'Tis as good a spot as any to rest and eat before we return to Aviemore." He touched her shoulder. "Shall we warm ourselves with a fire?"

While he kept his acolyte busy building the blaze Bhaltair slowly limped around the perimeter of the settlement. Oriana was yet too young and unlearned to sense the subtle traces of ancient spells, but once he finished his trek he was forced to agree with her. Whatever magic the Wood Dream might have used to protect themselves and their home, it had dissipated long ago. Gone too were the enigmatic spells they had once used to animate the totems that had transmuted into the *famhairean*.

He'd come hoping to find a trace of the magic, that he might use it to return the giants to their natural form.

Tired and heart-sick, Bhaltair sat with Oriana and pretended an appetite he didn't possess. The lass had gone to much trouble to prepare a fine meal of bread, cheese and pears poached in honey. As they ate he praised her for bringing a thickened mint brew that she diluted into a refreshing drink with their second flask of water.

"Grandfather always loved mint after a journey meal," Oriana confessed to him. "He said it eased the belly and cleared the mind."

Her charming anecdote reminded Bhaltair that he yet had another option to learn from the Wood Dream. In his young acolyte's head lay a powerful speak-seer talent that had provided much useful information since she'd come to him. He had also promised to train her to use and control it wisely, which he had yet to do. It pained him to use the lass this way, but the threat of the *famhairean* against mortal and druid kind outweighed all other concerns.

"My dear one, do you feel strong enough to attempt a channeling here?"

Her lips thinned as she glanced around them. "You wish me to reach out to the Wood Dream? I didnae ken any of these poor souls, Master, and they've been so long dead."

"Your gift doesnae have the limits that govern most others," he assured her. "You've but to reach out to the well of stars, and invite to you one of the tribe. Think on this place, and what you have seen. 'Twill draw them to you."

Oriana nodded reluctantly, and shifted herself into the kneeling position of a suppli-cant. Flattening her hands against the earth, she bowed her head. Her body trembled at first, but when she lifted her face again she went still, her eyes gone completely white.

"I would speak to the headman of the Wood Dream," Bhaltair said to her in a low, soothing voice. "We seek to ken the magics used by the tribe on the oak giants you created to protect the settlement."

She opened her mouth, and then jerked violently as fragmented words poured out of her in screeches.

"Romans...run you mustnae...coming for us...save the bairns...they're killing us they're killing—"

She broke off into a terrified scream and collapsed, writhing on the ground.

"*Oriana,*" Bhaltair yelled. He rushed to her, nearly falling in his haste, and turned her over onto her back. She convulsed, her hands digging into the soil and her limbs thrashing. "Come back to me, dear one. Release yourself!" When she didn't respond he slapped her cheek with a stinging swat, and her tearful eyes flew open. A wild look filled them but when they found his face he saw recognition set in. "Forgive me, lass."

"Oh, Master. They're so tormented. They're yet trapped in their own deaths. All of them came...all." She flung an arm over her eyes and burst into tears.

Bhaltair held her and comforted her, but even after she drifted to sleep the tears still slid down her splotched cheeks. He could not remember despising himself so much, even when he had tricked the last of his blood kin into a terrible trap.

"Yes, dear one, rest now."

He removed his cloak to cover her, and used her pack to pillow her head. He hoped no permanent damage had been inflicted on her by the violent channeling, but guessed she would wake feeling battered and frightened. He had seen some clusters of wild herbs on the fringe of the clearing, where the tribe must have once grown their spell garden. If he could find some valerian root and skullcap flowers, he could mix a potion to ease her bruised spirit and disperse her dread.

Sifting through the wild herbs, Bhaltair felt relieved to find the skullcap's purple flowers, now dry and withered from the cold, and a broad bunch of tiny white blooms that capped the valerian plant. Nipping enough flowers to make a single draft, he then unearthed the valerian with a practiced tug. As it came from the ground, something dropped at his feet. He grunted as he bent and plucked up the small oval of blackened wood. Time had rendered it as hard as stone, but had not yet scoured the marks carved inside the rims.

Bhaltair knew the old tribes had worn spell bands to collect power from Nature, and it made sense that the tribe would carve theirs from wood. He glanced over his shoulder at his slumbering acolyte before he pressed the oval against his heart. His own magic roiled up inside him, summoned by the nearness of the object.

The cuff still contained power.

With no small amount of trepidation, he slipped the oval over his hand and closed his eyes, opening himself and inviting in the ancient magic. At first it sparked angrily against his wrist—it sensed that he was not a member of the tribe—but then sifted through his flesh and met his own power.

The druid who had worn the cuff appeared in Bhaltair's mind, a tall, thin young man who tended the gardens. Like the old druid, he'd been harvesting valerian root, but not to calm a troubled mind. He mounded it in a basket filled with several other, very specific herbs and roots.

Bhaltair had gathered the same plants too many times to mistake their meaning. The Wood Dream's gardener had been preparing for a solstice ritual.

"Show me more," he muttered under his

breath, and sent a surge of his magic into the cuff.

The tribe gathered and then left the village, as the cuff absorbed the melodic sounds of their chanting in the clearing, and the magic which saturated it. But as the ritual came to its pinnacle, the chanting dissolved into screams of pain and terror. The cuff sensed the life of the gardener along with every other Wood Dream being snuffed out by the Romans. Even as its magic dwindled away, the wooden oval registered soldiers looting the settlement and slaughtering the livestock when the tribe's giant oak totems had come to life.

Bhaltair flinched as he saw the gruesome aftermath of the attack. The totems had converged on the invaders to crush them underfoot. They caught the soldiers who had tried to flee and tore them asunder. Finally, he saw why the legion had never again been seen after murdering the Wood Dream.

The totems opened the enormous maws of their mouths and stuffed the dead Romans inside, swallowing them whole.

Snatching off the oval, Bhaltair clutched it in his shaking fingers as he severed the connection to the cuff's magic. Now he understood why it seemed like the place still mourned the long-dead druids. The unfinished ritual had kept everything as it had been in the horrific moments of the tribe's demise. Until the spell to renew the land could be completed, nothing would change. To defeat the giants, it might require the last surviving members of the Wood Dream tribe to journey here and finish the solstice ritual.

Hendry Greum and Murdina Stroud would never do that.

Chapter Four

CADEYRN JERKED AWAKE to find himself in a dark room that smelled of a woman. His hands had been shackled to the bed posts above his head, and a slender body lay across his chest. The last thing he remembered was riding Dun Mor's perimeter, trying to tire himself enough to sleep without dreams. It seemed he had failed, for how else could he be with a pleasure lass? And why had she lain atop him so, when it was strictly forbidden? She must have been beaten by whoever stood watch...but he saw no one else in the room.

Since he'd be whipped bloody if he spoke to her, Cadeyrn arched his back, trying to dislodge her.

"Cade," she said, speaking his boyhood name as if they'd always known each other. When she pushed herself up he heard the clinking of chains, and saw the thin sunlight gild her tangled mane of streaked hair. "You're awake."

As the lady from his dreams rolled onto her side, a terrible confusion seized him. He had finished his training long ago. This could not be the tribe's compound. He'd not shared a bed with a female since joining his brothers as indentured warriors. There had been some fleeting time of freedom, and then a final battle with the *famhairean*. He had died there with the rest of his clan…and been awakened.

And yet he'd heard her voice before now, but when?

She sat up, and the light flickered over her pretty face. She'd already been beaten, badly and many times, judging by the color of her bruising. Cadeyrn wondered if somehow he'd been the cause of it.

"Are you all right then?" she asked, looking him over.

"Dinnae speak so loudly," he whispered to her in the barest murmur.

She lay down beside him, nestling close to put her mouth next to his ear. "They were waiting for us, boyo," the lady whispered.

Cadeyrn turned his head, and their faces brushed. Being in chains had already made him hard, as his body had been conditioned to expect sex when restrained. He could do nothing about the ferocious erection he sported, especially with her settled against his side.

He could hear her voice in his head. *Sorry,* she had said. No, something more. *Terribly sorry.*

"You took a nasty coshing," she said quietly and reached for the back of his head. She stroked her palm over his hair. "No blood, just a bit of a lump. How do you feel?"

He felt what any Skaraven in chains did: the urge to drag her atop him so she could ride his shaft, but her touch had aroused more than his errant cock. Cadeyrn felt his skinwork move as the inked owl opened its eyes, and a blue glow filtered through a rent in his sleeve. That it had only done so in battle made him try to shift away from her.

No choice.

"Your arm," she said, reaching out to the dim light. Before he could hiss a warning, she covered it with her hand, and the contact sent a wave of searing, undeniable hunger through his chest. "Cade, your *eyes*."

His battle spirit manifested by looking through him at her. It sent the low, thrumming sound it made when Cadeyrn fought well, and had pleased it. He saw a streak of its power shoot up over her wrist and arm to circle her nape and streak down to her other hand.

"Oh," she gasped and arched against him, shaking now. "Something…on my arms."

"Take your hand from me," he urged her, and when she did his skinwork stopped moving. "Dinnae touch my arm again." He took a calming breath. Though the woman of his dreams somehow lay next to him and had awakened his battle spirit, he had to push those thoughts aside. "What brought us here?"

"They hit you from behind and pushed us both into the portal. It brought us to where they've been holding me and the other women prisoner." She glanced around them. "This is a storage room in the mill, I think."

As she spoke he saw the tension in her

mouth. That tightness and the change in her eyes came from speaking falsehoods. None of his brothers lied to him, but he'd learned to detect it in others outside the clan. Yet why would she try to deceive him when they both had been captured?

Terribly sorry. No choice.

With but suspicion and a few strange words clamoring in his skull, he couldn't accuse her yet.

"Tell me your name."

"Lily Stover," she murmured. "You found me when I escaped. Do you remember anything?"

"Naught." The lie tasted bitter in his mouth. "How did you ken to find me?"

"I didn't." That was a truth. "I meant to return to my time." Another falsehood. "I'm so sorry about this."

And she was, Cadeyrn thought. Regret shadowed all of her words, which suggested she had been somehow compelled to deceive him.

"Tell me all that you've no' said. You can trust me, my lady."

Her mouth tightened. "Oh, I know

that, mate."

Before he could reply light poured into the room as the heavy door creaked open. A *famhair* with a scarred face trudged in. He tossed a bruised pear at Cadeyrn, smirking as the fruit bounced off his brow.

"Hendry want you." He reached for Lily.

"No," Cadeyrn said.

He fought his shackles, but he couldn't free himself. Instead he lay helpless as the giant yanked Lily's chains from the bed post, and tucked her under his arm. She struggled in vain as he carried her out and kicked shut the door.

Seeing her taken stilled Cadeyrn, and he craned his head to study the chains binding him to the bed. They had been wound around two posts, and looked old and rusted. He inspected each link until he found the two weakest, which connected the chains to his shackles. His arms burned as he poured all of his strength into twisting and pulling on the heavy metal manacles. It took long, painful minutes, but at last he pulled the links apart far enough to slip off the shackle rings.

He rolled off the bed, and quickly

inspected himself. His dagger and sword had been removed, along with the smaller dirk he kept tucked in his left boot. The mill room had been completely cleared out except for the bed, a bucket of water and some old rags. He considered smashing the bucket to create a weapon, but against the *famhairean* the largest stave of wood would be as useful as a twig.

Keeping his steps silent, Cadeyrn went to the door, which he discovered the scarred giant had neglected to bolt. Easing it open, he glanced outside. The passage that lay beyond appeared empty.

The sound of low voices drifted from the right end, drawing him out of the room.

He stayed to the shadows, measuring each step before he took it. The wood-rot stink of the giant grew stronger as he neared the end of the hall, where it opened into a larger space. Cadeyrn kept low against the wall, from where he could see but not be seen.

Lily sat at a table with a male druid in a dark blue robe. He held a steaming carafe, from which he poured brew into a mug sitting in front of her. Cadeyrn frowned. There were no giants and Lily appeared calm, almost bored.

"–did my best under the circumstances," she was saying. "Can't help that the portal botched things, and tore up my arms. Not as if I've been trained properly, like you lot."

"You saw no sign of Althea Jarden on the other side?" the druid asked, adding a dollop of honey to her mug.

"Didn't see anyone but the Skaraven chap, Hendry," Lily said. "I would have looked for their camp, but he insisted that I show him the portal. I couldn't let him go back and bring more men, then, could I?" She picked up the mug with her manacled hands and awkwardly took a sip. "They'd have made me bring them here and you'd have been in shambles."

"Indeed." Hendry sat back and watched her drink. "Then tell me, why did you take him?"

"I wasn't coming back with sod all. The Skaraven told me that the clan has Althea now. I can't tell you where they are. I've no clue where the portal dropped me, but Cadeyrn can. So." She put down the mug.

"Give us some time alone in that bed, and I'll have it out of him."

"How do you intend to persuade him to confide in you?" the druid countered. "After all, you did bring him here against his will."

"He doesn't remember that." She gave Hendry a cool look. "I'll persuade him with the one thing he really wants: my body."

The druid chuckled. "'Tis an inspired approach. Do all the females in your time barter their quims for what they want?"

"Don't be dull, Hendry. Women in my time do as we please. If we want a man, we have him." She smiled a little. "I could use a decent shag, and he's rather yummy. Even calls me 'my lady.'"

The gaps in Cadeyrn's memory vanished, along with every tender feeling he'd had for Lily Stover.

Terribly sorry about this, Cade. She'd said that after he'd been struck from behind, just as he'd fallen into the portal she'd opened. *No choice, really.*

His hands knotted into fists and his blood ran to boiling. So the lass had allied with the mad druids. Cadeyrn fought to ease his clenched jaw lest they hear his teeth grinding.

He'd known treachery in his boyhood. Because of it he'd taken a whipping that had nearly ended him. Yet this…this struck him to his core. He had dreamt of her nightly, and only now did he realize that he'd convinced himself that she was for him. His mouth drew into a tight line. He had naught to blame but himself. He'd seen dishonesty dance across her lovely face. Instead of trusting his battle spirit's sharp vision, he'd tried to believe the wench. Now he had to plan her defeat, and for that he would have to follow her example and make her believe he remained addled and trusting.

Lily might have made him a fool, but it would be her last deceit.

Cadeyrn slipped back down the passage and into the storage room, where he stretched out on the bed. Carefully hanging the rings of his shackles on the broken chain links before hiding the small gaps, he made it appear as if he'd never freed himself. Then he settled back and closed his eyes to summon a strategy.

Terribly sorry about this, Cade.

At least the Pritani headman who had

almost flayed him to his spine had never apologized.

As much as Cadeyrn despised Lily, he would not kill a female. Ending her life would afford him no advantage or pleasure. Once her scheme failed the mad druids would likely hand her over to their *famhairean* for sport. That he could not allow either. He had no druid blood, so he would need her to open the portal again. When he returned to Dun Mor he would turn her over to his chieftain for judgment. For her treachery Brennus wouldn't allow her to return to her future. He would probably give her to Bhaltair Flen for punishment.

The tree-knowers only *seemed* gentle. When it came to seeking justice, they could be as merciless as Romans.

Contemplating her fate made Cadeyrn hate himself. Why did the thought of her receiving her due make his gut knot? He had heard every traitorous word from her lips. She'd even jested about seducing him. He had to stop thinking of her as a lass and see her for what she was: a collaborator.

Sometime later a different *famhair* dragged

Lily back into the room. The giant's smooth face and flat eyes had more animation than the first. He inspected Cadeyrn for a long moment before he shoved Lily on top of him. Shackling Lily's wrist to a long chain, the giant secured the other end with a heavy lock to the side of the bed frame. Straightening and retreating a few steps, he watched them both.

"I'm all right," Lily said and lowered her mouth to his.

Cadeyrn knew what a kiss was—he'd watched his chieftain give many to Lady Althea—but accepting Lily's lips made him go hot and cold. She smelled of soap and tasted of honey and herbs, and the silky press of her mouth made him swallow a groan. This was why Brennus had refused to give his lady over to the druids, this melding, maddening delight that boiled over into hungry lust. He forgot the *famhair*, their chains and all that he knew as he tasted her with his tongue and felt hers caress the seam of his lips.

The sound of the giant leaving and the door being bolted made Lily go still. She lifted her head, and pressed her lips to his brow with something like affection.

"Sorry. I had to make that look convincing for Ochd."

She'd convinced the war master, and he knew what she was. "Why?" he demanded.

Lily scrambled off the bed. "I'd explain it all, but we don't have much time." She tested her chain, grimacing as the lock held. "How strong are you, boyo?"

"I cannae break iron," he told her, keeping his expression neutral. "Why did you kiss me?"

"So Ochd would see it. He'll report it to the nutters who grabbed us." She knelt down to study the lock. "Did Althea tell you about them?"

He wondered how many more lies she would tell him. "She spoke with my chieftain, no' me."

"Right. There are two of them. The man is named Hendry Greum, and he's with a woman called Murdina Stroud." She yanked on the lock and blew out a breath. "This is iron, too. Hendry and Murdina told us that they're druids from this time, and immortal, which I'm beginning to believe is true. They've plotted to get revenge on a bloke named Bhaltair Flen. They took us from the future because somehow we can help them with that."

Cadeyrn watched her climb back onto the bed, and controlled a flinch as she straddled his hips.

"What do you now, Lily?"

"I'm seeing if I can loosen your cuffs." She bent over him, and the moment she tugged on his shackle it came free. "Oh, fabulous. This chain is—"

He unhooked his other wrist and flipped over, trapping her under his body. Clamping his hand over her open mouth, he leaned close.

"You'll no' make a fool of me again, my lady. I broke out of my chains to come after you. I heard everything you promised the facking druid." Lily shook her head, her eyes wide. "Dinnae deny it. Now you'll answer my questions. 'Tis all you'll say. If you try to lie to me again, or scream for help, I'll gag you. Understand me?" As soon as she nodded he released her mouth. "Where do they hold the other lasses?"

"In the granary. It's west of the mill, behind the stables. There's only one way in, and they keep two guards on the door." She blinked a few times. "Please, Cade, let me explain."

"Only answers, or a gag," he reminded her. "Where lies the portal?"

"On the west side of the farm, in the woods." Her voice sounded defeated. "Only we prisoners can open it, so they don't bother guarding it. They have sentries surrounding the property, and Hendry sends out patrols at night."

Cadeyrn saw a tear slide down the side of her face into her hair. "Dinnae you dare weep, wench, after what you've done." He didn't want to ask her more, but the next question burst out of him. "How could you do this?"

"I did it to convince Hendry and Murdina to trust me," Lily said, averting her face. "I knew it was the only way they'd let me use the portal. So I lied to them, too." She closed her eyes. "If you're going to kill me have at it. Just promise me you'll free the others and get them away from those ruddy monsters."

Chapter Five

S ITTING AND WATCHING Perrin gobbling up a jam-smeared oat cake should have pleased Rowan, but she could hardly look at her sister anymore. Nor had she been able to swallow anything since the guards had started bringing them real meals. She looked at the food and saw Lily being dragged out of the granary to be executed. Out there somewhere the Brit lay in pieces, torn apart by Coig or Dha or maybe even the great prissy Aon, who hardly ever seemed to dirty his hands with anything.

Coig would have taken his time, Rowan thought. For some reason the sadistic guard had had it in for Lily from their first day in the

Ye Scotland of Auld. She could almost hear his scratchy, grating voice taunting her as he snapped bones and ripped flesh. He'd laugh as Lily wept, and screamed, and tried to crawl away—just as he had at the sheep farm.

Rowan didn't know which was worse: imagining the British woman's gruesome end, or knowing that her sister had made it happen. She still caught herself thinking up excuses for Perrin's betrayal. Fear—only Perrin hadn't been scared. Temporary insanity —but she'd sounded lucid and stable. Magic compulsion—yet Hendry hadn't cast a spill-the-beans spell on her. No, her perfect sister, whom everyone loved, who never did anything wrong, had simply traded Lily's life away to make things better for herself.

Perrin had calmly and deliberately sacrificed Lily on an altar of jam and oatcakes.

"They brought some cider today," Emeline said as she sat down beside her, a mug of juice in her hand. They'd been allowed to wash, and her clean hair practically glowed blue-black. "Would you like some? It's rather good."

"So was Lily," Rowan said tonelessly. "No thanks."

The nurse eyed Perrin for a moment before she said, "We've all been through so much, Rowan. Cannae you forgive her? I think Lily would."

"Lily can't do anything. Lily's dead. My sister killed her." She clenched her hands, digging her nails into her palms as her temper spiked. "I'm really not in the mood for talk therapy, Florence Nightingale. Go and enjoy the feast."

Emeline patted the swollen side of her face. "This has me on a cider-soaked bread diet, which I dinnae recommend at all. Nasty, mushy stuff."

Oddly, the nurse's Scottish accent seemed to be getting thicker by the day. She always tried to make light of their situation, too, which Rowan thought was utterly crass.

"Okay, I'll play," Rowan said. "What if Perrin had ratted you out? Would *you* forgive her for sending you to your death?"

"I hope I would. I was raised a Christian." Emeline touched her arm. "Drink a little juice for me, and I'll no' nag for the rest of the day."

Rowan took the mug, intending on pouring it out onto the floor. Her hand shook, something it never did, and her shrunken stomach made a feeble sound. A feeling came over her that reminded her of being on the beach, and soaking up the sun, two of Rowan's favorite things to do. She noticed the glitter of determination in the nurse's eyes, and thought of all the other times she'd felt good around Emeline. Basically, every time she stood within two feet of her. Everyone felt drawn to the nurse, Rowan realized. Even Perrin, who had always been notoriously shy around strangers.

"Stop using your mojo on me, Florence."

Emeline leaned closer. "Then stop acting like a bairn, you stubborn Yank. We need your strength."

She *was* acting like a brat, Rowan thought. *Don't hate me, Lily.* She chugged down the cider like bad tequila before she handed back the empty mug.

"If I puke, you're cleaning it up."

The nurse's expression turned rueful.

"Sensible notion, as I've plenty of practice." She hesitated before she added, "If you manage to keep it down, I've saved you bread and fruit, and some roast chicken." She smiled before she left her.

Her belly calming, Rowan watched Perrin finish eating and brush the crumbs from the front of her new outfit. The medieval dress hung from her as if she were a clothesline, and one good breeze would blow it off. She still looked beautiful in it. Perrin didn't know how to look ugly.

She doesn't know how to be *ugly,* Rowan thought.

Time flashed backwards as she remembered the first time she'd seen her older sister on stage. Perrin had been sixteen, and already obsessed with dance. Her ballet teacher had decided to do a production of Snow White, but had cast her own daughter as the princess. Perrin had been given the completely unsuitable role of The Evil Queen.

Perrin hadn't understood the character, or why she had hated her daughter's beauty. The concept of envy simply made no sense to her. In rehearsals she had struggled so much to portray the queen's murderous resentment that she'd nearly quit the production. Marion had finally sent her to take a crash course in acting with a former Broadway actress. The woman believed in big, overly-dramatic gestures that could be clearly seen by the audience even in the very back rows of the theater.

Acting gestures like the one she'd made to point out Lily.

Rowan didn't know she had walked over to her sister until she saw Perrin looking up at her with her big indigo eyes.

"Ready to beat the crap out of me now, Ro?" she asked, her tone serene.

It felt marvelous to grab the front of her sister's baggy new dress and use it to haul her to her feet.

"You conniving little sneak."

Emeline tried to get between them. "Rowan, dinnae do this."

"Shut up, Florence." Rowan used her other hand to hold the nurse back. To Perrin she said, "I saw you and Lily huddled together the other night. When I asked her about it she said she was just bitching at you to eat. It doesn't take an hour to do that. She *wanted* you to give her up. Why?"

"So she could get some help for us." Perrin glanced at the door. "Someone's coming. Don't ask about Lily, either of you. We're supposed to think she's dead."

Rowan released her as a middle-aged woman came in with two guards. Her still-sore back tensed at the sight of Murdina Stroud, who had whipped her unmercifully after their last escape attempt. The crazy half of the mad druid couple, the woman had the emotional stability of a rabid St. Bernard, and the heartfelt compassion of a serial killer. When Murdina wasn't bouncing between lightning bouts of sickening sweetness and homicidal rage, she hung all over Hendry, who seemed oblivious to her lunacy. Everyone else knew just how dangerous the woman could be. When Murdina smiled at Emeline, the nurse's face blanched.

"Fair morning to you, Healer." The druidess surveyed the remains of their meal. "I see you've been well fed. As you ken, my Hendry doesnae break his word." She turned to the biggest giant, and casually flapped her hand at Perrin. "Take that one to the mill."

Rowan got between Dha and her sister. "I can do whatever work you need done."

"Aye, and so you shall." Murdina came to her, and gave her shoulder a gentle pat. "You'll help Ochd repair our cart. 'Tis been overturned and broken." She seized Rowan by the neck and cut off her air. "Take the sister to the mill, Dha."

Rowan knew struggling would only earn her another punishment, but she didn't care. The moment she gripped the druidess's arm, however, her hands went numb and fell to her sides.

"Hendry cast a new body ward over me," Murdina said, smirking. "Naught can touch me but him and our *caraidean.* You'll do as I tell you, wee sister, or I'll whip the skin from the dancer's back."

When Rowan nodded, Murdina released her crushing grip. Coughing and gasping for air, she felt the cider starting to come back up, and swallowed until the feeling passed. Emeline looked ready to lunge at the druidess. Rowan felt another surge of affection for the gentle Scotswoman, who forgot to be placid and sweet whenever anyone was at bodily risk.

Emeline met her gaze, and Rowan felt a strange warmth roll over and wrap around her like a hug. Whatever the nurse's power was, it worked off emotions—and affected them, too.

"See you later," she told Emeline, and walked out of the granary with Murdina and Ochd.

Being in the sunlight made Rowan squint until her eyes adjusted. Murdina walked away from her and disappeared into the mill, while Ochd stood at her side and waited. Wood smoke hung heavily on the chilly air, but so did the scent of fresh-cut pine. She heard the sound of saws coming from behind the mill, and her stomach knotted as she thought of her sister.

"What is she going to do to Perrin?" Rowan asked, keeping her voice low.

"Lock her away from you. Make you help us." The guard gestured toward a heap of wood and wheels near the tree line. "Hendry needs cart."

From what she'd seen, Hendry used the guards for all the heavy lifting and carrying, so the cart had some other purpose. Probably to transport her, Perrin and Emeline to a place that didn't have a portal handy. Ochd might give her more details while she sabotaged the cart. Ochd liked to talk to her. But if she heard Perrin scream—

Rowan clenched her teeth until the urge to run into the mill passed. "Let's take a look at the damage."

Ochd accompanied her, even shortening his strides so their pace matched. Rowan noticed that unlike most of the other guards he'd worked on moving like a human being. His legs had hardly any puppet-like jerkiness now, and he even swung his arms as a man would, if the man were six and half feet tall and built like a front lineman with a steroids problem.

She eyed his profile and noticed something new. All of the guards had grids of tiny cracks all over their faces, as if their skin were made of clay that had been baked too long. When he turned his head to look at her she saw no cracks on the other side, either. His flesh tone had changed, too. Now he looked almost…human.

"Hendry make," Ochd said as they reached the cart.

"Make what?" She frowned at the broken wood and skewed wheels. "This mess?"

"Ochd." He lifted a huge hand and circled it in front of his nose. "Make me look human."

None of the guards spoke with much emotion, but he sounded almost proud. Even with the skin repair job, he really had no idea how strange he appeared, Rowan thought. What was more disturbing was how easily he'd guessed what she was thinking, and the fact that he'd just confirmed that he wasn't human.

"Okay." She was starting to get creeped out, so she focused on the cart. "How did this happen, anyway? Did Hendry drive this off a cliff?"

"Lily try to drop cart on him." Ochd tapped the side of his head. "Mind-mover."

The sous-chef had tried to dump this on the druid's head? Rowan glanced back at the granary.

"Really. What else did she do before he killed her?"

Ochd started to say something, and then scowled. "Murdina say fix cart. We fix."

"Sure," Rowan said.

She knew the guards were much smarter than they let on, and she didn't want to blow whatever scheme Lily and Perrin had hatched.

With the practiced eye of a carpenter, Rowan walked around the vehicle. She leaned over to inspect the primitive revolving front axle and the heavy transom, both of which remained intact. Everything had been made from tough, high-grained ash, the only reason it hadn't collapsed in a pile of splinters.

"This has four wheels, so technically it's a wagon, not a cart." She crouched down to look underneath the bed boards, and then stood. "Two of the wheel hubs have cracked, and all of the side ladders are snapped off. We need to shore up the wheels, turn it over, and then I'm going to need some– *Wait.*"

With a single heave Ochd turned over the wagon. A splintering groan came from beneath the bed as it landed, and the two damaged wheels collapsed.

"Great." Rowan closed her eyes for a moment. "Thanks."

"Wheels arenae sound." Ochd kicked one, which cracked in two and fell apart.

"I appreciate that opinion, but I'm not a wheelwright."

Even as she said that, Rowan could see how the spokes had been fitted to the rims, and the simplicity of the hubs. She hadn't seen any ash trees yet, but there were some big elms that might serve. Her fingers always itched whenever she thought of wood-working, but she also felt the hair on the back of her neck prickle.

Turning around helped Rowan dodge a fist-sized stone whizzing toward her face. A second one bounced off her shoulder, and then something bigger rammed into her. With the wind knocked out of her, she went flying through the air to land at Ochd's feet with a painful thud.

"Want her first," Coig said. The worst of the guards, loomed over Rowan. "Teach her ken her place."

Ochd hefted Rowan up from the ground, tucking her under his hard arm. "Murdina say she mend cart. You beat her, she cannae work."

"Make healer work," Coig said as he approached, his hands outstretched. "Give her to me."

Rowan remained perfectly still as she stared up at the guard's flat, hate-filled eyes. His face had cracked so badly that pieces of it were flaking off, revealing underneath an uneven, blackened grain like moldy wood. His big, yellowed teeth had split on all the edges as well, making him look as if he had a mouthful of huge splinters.

"You rot," Ochd said as Coig reached for Rowan. "Go to Hendry. He fix you."

The other guard stopped in his tracks, and peered at Ochd. "Fix me." He made a grating sound as his jaw worked, grinding his broken teeth together. "Naught fix me." With one last glare at Rowan he turned around and trudged back toward the mill.

Only when Coig was out of sight did Ochd put Rowan on her feet. This wasn't the first time he'd protected her from that bastard.

"Why did you do that?"

"Hendry promise treat you well. Coig forget." The guard gestured at the broken wagon. "What we need to fix?"

"Wood for the wheels and side ladders. Tools." She glanced at the mill. "Somewhere to work away from Coig. Is Hendry the only reason you're protecting me?"

"No." He gave her a long look before he said, "We go mark trees. I cut later. Come."

Hardly believing her luck, Rowan followed him to the forest trail and into the woods. They were heading straight toward the portal, Rowan realized, which Lily had probably run to when she'd dropped the cart. The portal which she herself could open with just a touch, jump in, and get the hell out of–

You can't leave Perrin behind, Marion's voice whispered in her head. *You must protect your sister.*

Rowan had always detested her adoptive mother, but never more so than in that moment. Here she had the perfect opportunity to escape, to go back to her time, go get help, or just whizz off to another place in Scotland. And still Perrin had to come first.

"Which trees do we cut?" Ochd asked, startling her out of her thoughts.

"For the straight pieces we'll need elm." Thinking of Perrin filled her with so much separation anxiety she asked, "You're going to bring my sister back to the granary after I fix this, right?"

The guard shook his head. "Murdina keep her, to make you fear. To make you afraid," he corrected himself.

"Can you get her out of the mill, and bring her to me?" Before he could reply she said, "You can tell them that we need more help with repairing the wagon."

"I cannae lie to Wood Dream." He took out a dagger and used it to gouge an X on the trunk of a large elm. "I willnae allow them or Coig harm…to harm you, Rowan."

He was actively trying to sound human now. When he offered her the dagger she gripped it tightly.

"I can't hurt you with this," Rowan said, looking down at the short blade. "That's why you're giving it to me."

"No. I give to you so you can mark trees," he told her. "I find the ash wood."

If she could get Ochd on their side, Rowan thought, they might actually have a chance of surviving.

"Okay. Let's mark trees."

It took another hour to find enough mature elms for the project, and toward the end the guard actually located an ash tree deep in the woods. The tree had recently died, probably from a lightning strike, judging by the black burned streak bisecting the trunk.

"We can steam this wood to curve it into new wheel rims," Rowan said as she marked it. Since she had no further use for the blade, she handed it back to Ochd. "That's all we need."

Ochd nodded and accompanied her out of the forest. In the mill yard several guards were leading some horses to a trough, which Tri was filling with a bucket.

They always made the stupid one carry the water, Rowan thought. She couldn't help letting out a short laugh as the scar-faced guard lost his balance and fell into the trough. The other guards quickly backed away to avoid Tri's splashing efforts to right himself.

"You need to get Hendry to fix him," Rowan muttered to Ochd.

"Naught can do that." The guard sounded impassive, but his new face grimaced.

Finally pushing himself out of the trough,

the scar-faced guard grinned down at himself. "Tri wet. Tri like better than burnt."

He didn't like it for long. Huge tumors began bulging all over the guard's scarred face and neck, extruding into pear-shaped knots that rapidly swelled and began falling off his body.

Rowan remembered the horrific whipping she'd taken from Murdina, and how Ochd had held her against the post for the duration. She'd tried to keep silent during the lashing, but she couldn't stop the tears of agony from running down her face. When one had plopped on Ochd's palm, a twig had sprouted from it. He'd even told her to bite it to keep from screaming.

Water did something to them that they didn't like.

"Go see Aon," Dha shouted at Tri, who swatted at the pears hanging under his chin as he lumbered toward the back of the mill.

The rest of the guards retreated from the trough and the puddles around it. Three led the obviously-thirsty horses back toward the stables.

Rowan thought for a moment. She'd never

CADEYRN81

seen any of the guards go near water. Even in the granary they stayed far away from their drinking and bathing buckets, which Hendry always carried in.

Water is their weakness.

Chapter Six

LILY FELT CADEYRN roll away from her and braced herself for what was to come. When the bed creaked, she opened her eyes to watch him move to stand by the door. He seemed to be listening for sounds from the passage. Why was he turning his back on her when he thought she worked for the druids? She wanted to ask, but the consequences of what she'd done were finally settling in. It took all her attention to hold back the shakes and tears. Closing her eyes, she thought of the last time she'd felt this wretched.

Back in London, on the day she'd left her father's house.

Lily had waited until she'd taken her bag

out to the cab she'd called before she went into her father's library. She could have left her keys with the housekeeper, but that felt cowardly. The therapist she'd been secretly seeing for more than a year had advised her to begin her new life by leaving all the family's dirty linen with her father.

The library smelled of old leather, older books, and brandy-soaked dried apricots, Edgar Stover's favorite snack. A pile of the dark, withered fruit sat in a crystal bowl on his large, immaculate desk. Behind his custom-designed executive chair hung a painting of Charlotte, Lily's dead mother. Her father hadn't looked up from his copy of The Daily Telegraph.

"I see you're determined to continue this farce," he said.

Edgar's bulk always seemed to grow larger with every moment Lily looked at him, but at twelve stone the epicure dwarfed most men. Although he sounded calm, she could see the redness flagging his round cheeks, and the slight quiver of his double chin. He never showed this side of his temper in public, or someone might have meddled. Convincing the world that he was an elegant, refined gent meant a great deal to Lily's father. He went to a great deal of trouble to perpetuate that façade.

"I must report for duty in an hour." She'd never again have to cower in front of him, and the thought dispelled her own shakes. "There's a great deal of work to be done before the passengers arrive. We sail tomorrow at noon."

He snapped down the upper half of his newspaper. "I suppose as your current employer I should have the honor of firing you. I believe I will, for theft, and I'll inform your—What is it called again? Cruise line?—that you're not to be trusted."

"Oh, dear, my letter must have gone astray. I officially resigned as your sous-chef last week." She tossed the letter onto his desk. "I also mailed copies to the cruise line and my new supervisor."

Her father chuckled. "Do you imagine that they'll take your word over mine? I own the best restaurants in London. You're a glorified scullery maid."

"I included a copy of the video from the last time you treated me like one." She rolled up her sleeve to show him the results. "My new boss is an executive chef. He'll recognize the mark and how I got it."

Edgar's brow lowered. "Codswallop. You got in my way that night."

"I was on the other side of the kitchen when you began screaming at me for using dill instead of tarragon for your quail." She nodded at the envelope. "I thought your memory might be spotty, so I included a copy of the video for you. You really should have checked the security cameras before you got cross, Daddy."

He peered at the envelope and then her. "You planned all this, didn't you? You switched the cameras on early that night, and then deliberately provoked me."

She had no qualms about admitting her part. "I'm well aware of how much you despise dill with game birds. I made sure to add lots, just in case you'd drunk too many cocktails before eating. According to your last article for Fine Cooking, alcohol does so dull the palate."

His eyes turned to dark crescents. "I'll

make it my business to ruin you. You won't get a job frying fish and chips in Brixton."

"I'm never coming back to England." As he lumbered to his feet she played her final card and pulled the boning knife out of her sleeve. "Lay a finger on me, Edgar, and you'll dearly regret it."

Though he came up on his toes and leaned forward, he stopped, eyes on the blade. His mouth twisted in a cruel curve.

"How like your mother you are," he sneered. "Weak. Go on then, just leave."

"Mummy committed suicide after taking years of your shite," she snapped. "You only waited a few months after the funeral before you started in on me. You forced me to become a chef. You wouldn't let me work anywhere but your restaurants. You've kept me locked up in this bleeding mansion for years, and even that wasn't enough to please you. Well, I got help, Daddy, and I'm not going to hang myself. I'm going to live, far from here, away from you."

Turning her back on him had been a terrible risk, but Lily couldn't look at him anymore. He followed her out into the hall, where he stood watching her walk to the front entry.

"If you go, we're finished," Edgar had roared after her. "Shag your way across the Atlantic, you scheming little slut, but you'll get nothing again from me."

"Please, God, yes." She yanked open the door and stepped outside to her first moment of freedom in twenty-six years. London's gloomy charcoal sky had actually looked beautiful.

Lily opened her eyes to see the rough beams of the ceiling over the bed. She'd fallen asleep, and when she looked for Cadeyrn she saw him sitting by the bed with his eyes closed. His streaked dark hair, so unlike hers, framed his handsome, clever face. His mouth had relaxed from a hard, grim line to a sensual fullness. When he slept he looked tantalizing, like a lover waiting for his lady to wake him with a kiss.

He might have been her lover, if she hadn't cocked up everything.

She'd never regret what she'd done to get away from Edgar, Lily thought, but she wished she had been honest from the start with the

Scotsman. She'd been so afraid that if she had told him the truth, he wouldn't have come back with her to rescue the others. She hadn't even given Cade a chance.

Or maybe I'm just as manipulative as Edgar, Lily thought tiredly. Not that it mattered anymore. Once the big Scottish warrior decided on a plan, he'd throttle her and that would be her end. At least she'd gotten away from her father for a few months. The only part she hated was that Edgar would assume after she'd gone missing in her time that it was because of the solicitor's letter. Her father would go to his grave thinking she'd jumped off the ship in despair over him.

At least she'd have the kiss with Cadeyrn to take with her into the unknown. Lily could still taste him on her lips, as heady as champagne and twice as intoxicating. She'd never had any relationships. Edgar had scared off the boys in school who had taken a fancy to her. But she'd had one lovely, lusty affair with a Norwegian helmsman. That had ended when he'd taken a job on another ship. He'd even asked her to put in for a transfer, but she'd known she was too damaged for such a fun-loving bloke. Cade, now, he might have been her proper match.

"Lily."

She looked over, flinching a little as she saw Cadeyrn kneeling by the bed. She tried not to look at his hands. "Sorry I fell asleep, mate. Treachery can be so exhausting. How long was I out?"

"All day." He studied her face. "Why do you call me 'mate'?"

"It's what we call chaps we like in my time. It means friend. So does boyo, although that's a bit cheekier." Why would he let her sleep instead of killing her? Oh, he meant to leave her behind for the nutters. Hendry would make short work of her, unless he tossed her to Coig. "Ready to go, then?"

"No' without you." He reached down, giving the lock on her chains a sharp twist to the left. His eyes never left hers. "I dinnae trust you, but I'll need your help. When we return to my clan, you'll be judged by my chieftain."

Lily's throat tightened. He wouldn't kill her, and that was the best thing that had happened since she'd been dragged back through time. *No, kissing him was.*

"What can I do?"

He didn't answer, but his arm bulged, and he grunted as the sound of metal groaning and wood splintering came from the side of the bed.

"Allow me," she said.

She pushed a small amount of her power at the lock and felt a prick of pain behind her right eye. He pulled up the chain, showing a broken link hanging from the end.

"You did this?"

Lily nodded. "I can move things with my thoughts. I made one link come apart."

"You can do this to anything?" When she nodded his expression grew grim. "Why didnae you use it on the *famhairean* to escape?"

"I did, at the forest farm, to help Althea." She considered telling him about the after effects, but so far the discomfort had been manageable. "It winks out on me if I use it too much or too often. After the battle I could barely roll a pebble for days." And she'd had a gusher of a nosebleed that it had taken Emeline an hour to stop.

"Then dinnae use it," Cadeyrn said flatly.

"Until we reckon how to escape, we let them believe I've fallen for your scheme."

So, he was going along with it. Relief made her voice shake a bit as she said, "We still need a plan, and I have to get word to the others, so they'll be ready."

His eyes narrowed. "You cannae help them if you're dead."

"There are other ways, boyo— I mean, Cade." She bit her lip as she rose from the bed, and reached under it to take out the dagger she'd stolen from him. "Sorry. I slipped this from your belt after we came through the portal."

Cadeyrn's jaw tightened. "How many *famhairean* did the druids bring here?"

"All of them, about fifty, I think." She handed him the dagger, which he tucked in his sleeve. "Hendry keeps guards outside on all the doors at night, but there's a window in the kitchen that looks out on the garden. We can use that to get out and back in."

He thought for a long moment. "I cannae risk being caught outside. The *famhairean* will ken you have betrayed their masters and kill us both."

"Then I'll go alone." She sat up, gingerly easing up her leg to examine the shackle, which still had a short length of chain attached to it. Carefully she wove the links around the cuff. "They'll make noise," she explained. "Now how do we get out of this mess, and what do I tell the other women?"

Before he could reply the sound of heavy footsteps came from the outer passage.

"Quickly," Cadeyrn said.

She latched her shackle to the broken chain, and moved over so he could join her on the bed. She straddled him to push his hands up to the head board, and hooked them in place just as the door opened.

Lily bent down. "I'm sorry about this," she whispered by his ear. "But we have to make them believe I'm seducing you."

Cadeyrn tensed under her. "Then kiss me again."

Lily cradled his face between her palms and covered his mouth with hers. She shifted down so she could lay atop him, her thighs pressed against the outside of his. He went erect against her, so hard and so fast it made her gasp against his lips. Then a shadow fell over them, and she turned her head to look up at the guard. It was Ochd, and he was staring at them both with an odd intensity.

"What do you want?" Lily demanded, trying her best to sound cross. "We're busy."

"I bring food." He dropped a loaf and a wedge of cheese on the bed. "What do you to him?"

"I'm thanking him for not being a complete arse, like you lot," she snapped. "Now if you could please sod off?"

"You thank with mouth-on-mouth…kissing?" Ochd asked her, reaching as if to touch her face.

Lily swatted his hand away. "I'm not thanking you for anything, you ruddy wazzock. You've barely brought enough food for him. Get out."

The guard scowled, but shuffled back and left.

She waited until Ochd bolted the door before she pushed herself up. "We'll have to do more of that if we're to make them think we're shagging. Sorry, I mean–"

"I ken what you mean. Dinnae be sorry." He watched the door for another moment before he asked, "Do you ever speak to the *famhairean* with such contempt?"

"More or less. I've gotten beaten for it, but it was worth the bruises." The warm rush of his breath on her face made her want to hold onto him. But more than anything she wanted to lose herself in his gorgeous golden eyes, the ones that had helped her keep her sanity. Instead she climbed off and took down his manacles before she collected the food. "Here, you must be hungry."

"Aye, but no' for that." He got off the bed. "Tell me about the other lasses they've taken, and what powers they possess."

"There's a Scottish nurse named Emeline, and two Americans, Rowan and Perrin. They're sisters." She described them briefly before she said, "Emeline has been doctoring us, and she's very good at calming hot tempers. I think she can influence feelings. Rowan has a scorching temper, but she's very strong, likely because she's a carpenter. Her power is a bit like mine. She can change the shapes of wood. Perrin is a dancer, but she's been under the weather... ah, sickly. She has visions of things before they happen. She saw me finding you by the river."

Cadeyrn nodded. "Did she see us escape?"

"No." Lily grimaced. "She can't control her visions at all. They simply pop into her head whenever they like. She's become very frail, so we've tried to protect her from them." She caught the shift in his expression. "What is it?"

"The *famhairean* despise all humans, but they serve the mad druids. 'Twas their tribe that first created them. They'll do much to protect Hendry and Murdina—and that we can use. But we'll need time, mayhap a day." He used his dagger to divide the cheese and bread, and put half in her hands. "Eat."

Lily had no appetite, but she dutifully pinched off a piece to chew. Broken bits of grain studded the stale bread, and the cheese proved almost as hard. But sitting and eating with Cadeyrn made her feel a strange rush of emotion. She didn't understand it. Being close to him made her feel safe, and she'd never felt that way around the opposite sex.

"Tell me your thoughts," he said suddenly.

She could have said anything, but the truth

suddenly came out of her. "I'm glad you didn't kill me, as I haven't had a lot of luck with men. I don't trust them."

"Before Althea came to the clan, I'd never spoken to a woman." Lily blinked at him, but he got up and went to the door to peer through the narrow gap by the hinges. "They've put out the lights."

"Stay on the bed while I'm gone," Lily told him, mounding the blanket over his tartan to make it look as if she lay beside him. When she reached for his shackles to help arrange them, he caught her hand in his.

"If you're caught, run for the portal. My clan shall find you." Before she could argue he shook his head. "If you dinnae return I'll free the other lasses and follow."

He'd be torn apart or beaten to death before he reached the granary, Lily thought, and he knew it. "I'm not leaving anyone behind here. We go together, or not at all."

His expression darkened. "You'd wager your life on that?"

"I have already, mate. Twice."

She went to the door, and used her power to lift the bolt bar, catching it as she stepped through and easing it back into place. The needle of pain behind her eye expanded into a throbbing knot, and her vision blurred. Blinking until it passed, Lily tread silently down the passage and looked into the empty kitchen. Getting through the window without making a sound took several tense minutes. She dropped down into the garden, landing on a patch of snow-covered earth that crunched beneath her ruined shoes. The soles split and flopped as she tried to walk.

I'm not going to die because of bloody useless shoes.

Lily took her stockinged feet out and hid the shoes behind the wood pile. Crouching over, she made her way through the dead plants in the garden until she reached the edge, and peered out into the yard. Giants stood sentry at every door leading into the mill, but they'd all gone into what she thought of as their sleep mode, standing still with their eyes closed. As long as she didn't make any sound she wouldn't rouse them.

It still took all her nerve to pad silently over to the blocked door of the granary. Several rocks bruised her toes and heels along the way, but the cold soon numbed her feet. She didn't have the strength to move the big mill stone the druids had used to block the granary's door. Pushing the heavy wheel aside with her power would also make noise, so instead she shifted it at an angle away from the door and held it there as she slipped inside. Once out of sight she wedged it back in place.

Out of the shadows Rowan appeared, a spear in each hand.

"It's okay, Florence," the carpenter said, lowering the weapons. "Stover's come back from the dead."

Lily found herself being hugged by the carpenter, which oddly didn't bother her in the slightest.

"Perrin promised she'd let you know," Lily told her.

"She never got the chance. Murdina took her and locked her up." Rowan stepped back and grinned at the wide-eyed nurse. "We go get my big sis, and then we're out of here."

"Not quite yet." Quickly Lily explained the situation. "Cade and I need another day to work out a diversion. Be prepared to go as soon as the sun sets. Where are they keeping Perrin?"

"Maybe somewhere in the mill," Emeline said and squinted at Lily's face. She took a piece of rag from her pocket. "You've another nosebleed, lass."

"Thanks." She blew and mopped up, but the bleeding had already stopped. "Rowan, can you get word to Perrin, or find out exactly where they're keeping her?"

"I think they've got her in the wood shed behind the mill," the carpenter said. "It's the only place Ochd wouldn't let me go near while we were working on the wagon. You did a number on it, by the way."

"The old cart I dropped?" When Rowan nodded Lily frowned. "Why would he have you fix it? They'd already begun taking it apart before me."

Rowan's smile faded. "Murdina dragged Perrin away to force me to help Ochd fix it. She threatened to whip her if I didn't."

"Maybe she's testing you," Emeline said. "To learn what sort of power you have. They never saw what you did at the forest farm."

"Yeah, that has to be it." Rowan looked

oddly shaken. "Anyway, what else do you need us to do before tomorrow night, Lily?"

She eyed the spears the other woman still held. "Make more of those, and would you give me and Emeline some privacy? I need her advice about a medical problem."

Rowan nodded and retreated to the back of the granary. Once she was out of earshot Lily explained to the nurse her only other concern.

"He could be lying," Emeline admitted. "But you'd find out the truth only after it's too late to stop it."

"He's made lots of threats, but this...this sounded real." Lily nodded to herself. "Please don't tell anyone. I'll deal with it once we're safe."

Chapter Seven

UNABLE TO SLEEP, Ruadri Skaraven rose from his pallet and dressed in darkness scented by sage smoke. He'd cleansed his private chamber thrice since returning to Dun Mor, and still it felt more like a coffin than a room. No matter how many torches he lit, shadows lingered in nooks and crannies like so many dark eyes, watching and waiting. Ruadri had long resisted his guilt over being a spy for the druids, telling himself that he could use it to benefit and protect his brothers. Since awakening to immortality, however, the weight of his never-ending betrayal had grown crushing. He'd bear the burden, but Gods, what he would give to have one moment free of it.

In Ruadri's mind he saw the lovely pale face of the black-haired healer who had been stolen from the future. Every time he imagined her she seemed to be reaching out to him, as if she knew his pain and the cure for it. He'd give anything to save her, even his own worthless life. Daily he implored the Gods to watch over her.

Mayhap they shall treat her kindlier than me.

Out in Dun Mor's great hall Ruadri encountered Brennus speaking quietly with a group of clansmen dressed for patrol duty. He waited until the men dispersed before he approached the chieftain, who looked grim.

"What trouble now?" he asked Brennus.

"Our war master never returned to the stronghold last night," the chieftain said. "Taran came to me this morning after he found Liath's stall empty, but you ken how Cade goes off alone when he broods. I reckoned he went by water to the McAra. He's been thick with the laird, and Maddock would have bid him stay for a meal and mayhap the night. I just had word from the laird. Cade never came to him."

"'Tis no' like Cadeyrn to leave Dun Mor

without word to any of us." Ruadri thought for a moment. "He's no' been the same since your lady returned to life. Mayhap he's gone to his old watch blind. 'Twas where he went as a mortal when he wished for solitude."

"Does it yet stand?"

Ruadri nodded. "'Tis no' that far from here, and Cadeyrn may need my counsel, if you'll permit me."

"My thanks, Brother," Brennus said and touched his shoulder to the shaman's.

Ruadri went first to the stables to speak with Taran, who confirmed that their war master had taken his mount and ridden out to check the perimeter.

"'Twas an excuse," the horse master said, "as 'tis been most nights. Cadeyrn doesnae sleep well of late." He eyed him. "Nor do you, it seems."

"'Tis dreams plaguing Cadeyrn?" Ruadri asked, and saw Taran's shoulders lift and fall. "Still the keeper of the clan's secrets. Tell me this much: 'tis anything harmful to our war master or the clan?"

"I dinnae ken. He doesnae confide so much in me as you reckon." The other man hesitated before he said, "But every night past, he's returned by dawn. No' this morning. 'Tis no' like him, Ru. Even if he wished to remain alone another day, he'd have brought back his mount for feeding."

Ruadri decided to follow the trail on foot, and headed to where Cadeyrn would have begun his ride. In the low slant of the morning light, he found faint hoof prints in the soft soil by the lower slopes, and followed them to the river. A rustling in the brush made Ruadri draw his blade, until a gray stallion, saddled but riderless, emerged and slowly walked over to him.

"Liath." Ruadri sheathed his blade and checked the horse for wounds. From the mud marks on the animal's legs and belly, and the dampness of the saddle, the stallion had been wandering for some time. He found the bridle intact, and no sign that Liath had broken from tether. "Cadeyrn would never leave you out here for the night."

Ruadri checked the ground until he found boot marks leading into the river. He left Liath and crossed the water. On the other side he found where Cadeyrn had walked up the bank and stood long enough to leave deeper prints. A confusion of tracks beyond it separated into two distinct sets. The smaller bore a strange, flat sole on one side, and the imprint of toes on the other. None of the clan had such small feet, and the shape suggested the tracks belonged to a female.

How could a lass have come…?

He snapped his head up to stare in the direction the tracks led off, and hurried through the trees to the stone mounds that protected one of his own, oldest secrets. Magic still lingered in the air from the recently opened portal. Ruadri sat down on the enclosing stones that he himself had carried and placed to conceal the old sacred grove. He'd even long ago planted pines to disguise the oaks that powered the portal. None of the clan knew about the spot. Brennus would have come to him immediately if they'd discovered it. That meant someone had come out of the portal and lured Cadeyrn here to take him through it. A druidess with a strange shoe. She had to be one of the lasses the *famhairean* had brought back from the future with Althea.

Ruadri looked up at the oaks, and felt the

pull of their silent, ancient power. The Gods had demanded much of him, but this?

"What would you have me do? Confess all now, and let Brennus take my head? I cannae go through to rescue Cadeyrn and the lasses. Not alone, and I dinnae ken where they are." He bunched his hands into fists and struck the weathered rock. "You would take all from me and give me naught."

As if in response, the portal in the center of the grove slowly whirled opened.

Ruadri scrambled backward, falling to the ground with a thud. Cursing under his breath, he pushed himself upright and marched away from the grove. Once he crossed the river, he took hold of Liath's reins and mounted him.

"I'm no' ready to die," he muttered. "But when I do, it shall be by my choosing."

Back at the stables, Ruadri told Taran that he'd found the horse wandering alone, and then made his way into the stronghold. There he found whiskey and drank until his gut unknotted an inch.

"Never tell me you've taken to the bottle," an amused voice said.

Ruadri turned around to look into the

black eyes of Kanyth, the clan's weapons master and Brennus's half-brother. New burns marred his big hands, and his leather work apron bore smoke and spark marks. He'd taken to working in his forge at night, likely to exercise his battle spirit, which was among the most powerful in the clan—and bitingly cruel.

"Cadeyrn's gone missing," Ruadri said. "I found his mount by the river." Tired of his own endless lies, he took another swallow before he said, "I found two sets of tracks that led me to a concealed sacred grove. There's a portal there that someone opened, and 'twasnae Cadeyrn."

All the amusement vanished from the Weapon Master's handsome face. "I'll fetch Brennus."

Kanyth returned a short time later with the chieftain and his mate. Lady Althea had dressed in some of her garments from her own time, and had tied back her bright red hair in a long tail. Drowsiness should have softened her crystalline blue eyes, but instead they looked like the shadows in ice.

She came directly to Ruadri, her slender

frame almost vibrating with tension. "Someone took Cade?"

"'Twould seem so, my lady." He regarded the chieftain. "I found two sets of tracks leading to this portal: Cadeyrn's and a smaller tree-knower, likely female. I reckon she lured him to it. Mayhap 'twas this Murdina Stroud your lady described to us."

"No," Althea told him. "The druids and the giants can't access the portals. It had to be one of the other women they took from the future." She grimaced. "But how could they know where we are?"

Ruadri had some ideas, but to confess them would reveal too much knowledge of how the portals worked. "I cannae tell you, my lady."

"We shall look at this grove, then," Brennus said and turned to his mate. "You may go with us, but you willnae reopen the portal."

"I don't know how," she admitted. "Even if it opened it might decide to dump me back to my own time. Then I'd just have to jump back here again."

The chieftain dragged her close and gave

her a brief but passionate kiss. "You go nowhere without me, Wife."

At the stables Taran had mounts waiting, and joined them on his own golden-maned white mare. Not for the first time did Ruadri envy the horse master for the way he rode, as if he and his mount were one creature. Taran also looked worried now, and since his power over horses included some mystical properties, he imagined Liath had provided more than proof of Cadeyrn's disappearance.

Ruadri rode up alongside Taran. "What did the stallion tell you?"

"He smelled blood," the horse master said. "Fresh, but druid, and female."

"An injured tree-knower." Ruadri frowned. "Mayhap she escaped them."

The horse master shook his head. "If she had, she'd never have gone back with Cade. They'd have sent her as an enticement."

Once they reached the river they dismounted and tethered the horses. Brennus scooped up Althea in his powerful arms before he crossed.

"A little river water won't hurt me, you

know," she grumbled as he set her on her feet. "Not like I can ever get sick again."

"Indulge me," he said and tugged on the raven ring she wore around her neck. "I yet remember you in your last moments as a mortal."

"Frozen solid, yeah, that was romantic." Althea shuddered before she looked at the ground around them. "Wait." She crouched down to peer at the smaller set of tracks, and then gazed up at her mate. "I've seen this footprint before, when we were being held at the forest farm. This is Lily's shoe. They're a particular brand that chefs wear at work, to protect their feet."

Following the tracks to the hidden portal, Ruadri considered telling Brennus all. If he did, he could offer to open the portal for them, and use his druid knowledge to lead them directly to the *famhairean's* new location. That he would have to kill himself or be executed as a traitor didn't worry him. He'd accepted long ago that choosing an unhappy death would be his recompense for a lifetime of betrayal.

Or he could use this revelation to end his wretched servitude to the tree-knowers for good, and none of his brothers ever had to know what he'd done.

"Chieftain, if you'll allow, I'd seek counsel from Bhaltair Flen," Ruadri said carefully. "He has much knowledge of these portals. He may advise us how to find Cadeyrn and the ladies yet held by the mad druids."

Althea frowned at him. "You think the old man can tell us how to use the portal as some kind of tracker?"

"I cannae say what he may ken, my lady." He kept his expression bland as he regarded the chieftain. "'Twould serve his purpose to have us pursue the giants. I reckon that would prod him to advise me."

Brennus hated Bhaltair Flen, and it showed in his tight jaw and glittering eyes. "Very well, but dinnae tell more than necessary to gain his insight. I'll no' have him meddling with the clan again. Taran, round up two patrols, and put them here to keep watch. I dinnae want this portal left unattended until we've Cade back home."

Chapter Eight

L ILY LEFT THE granary, replaced the millstone against the door and crept back through the garden. She remembered to grab her shoes before she climbed through the kitchen window. What little energy she had left ebbed as she slipped back into the storage room. Using her power one more time to secure the bolt bar, she staggered over to the bed.

"You're hurt," Cadeyrn said and caught her and held her on his lap, his arms cradling her. "What did they do?"

"Nothing. No one saw me. It's just another headache." It felt so good to rest her cheek against his shoulder as she told him about the other women and what they had said. The only thing she held back was what she had discussed with Emeline. "When the time comes they'll be ready, but if Rowan can't get Perrin out of the wood shed–"

"We'll free her." His hand smoothed her hair back from her face. "Dinnae fret."

"That's all I've been doing since I landed here." For some reason she couldn't keep her eyes open. "When I've not been dodging fists and trying to stay warm. All right if I nod off for a few hours?"

Cadeyrn lowered her onto her side, and reached over her to attach her ankle cuff to the chain. He then stretched out behind her, tugging her back against him.

"Sleep," he said. "I'll keep watch."

Lily forgot about her miserably pounding head as his soothing body heat slowly thawed her chilled limbs. He'd been so kind to her, and he had absolutely no reason to be that. Despite being afraid of the answer, she couldn't stop herself.

"Do you hate me, Cade?"

The silence stretched to an eternity as she held her breath.

"No, lass," he said quietly. As he tucked his arm around her waist, she exhaled and then covered her mouth to stop from crying in relief. "I ken why you deceived me. 'Tis only that it reminded me of another betrayal."

She sniffed. "You met another woman from the future when you were a boy?" she tried to joke.

Behind her, Cadeyrn shook his head. "I caught a Pritani lad eating the bread he'd been sent to deliver for me and my brothers. 'Twas a desperate time. The crops had failed, and everyone went hungry."

She rolled over to face him. "Did you give him some food?"

"My share, aye." His gaze grew distant. "He begged me no' to tell, as he'd be lashed for stealing. His fear persuaded me to promise my silence. The next morn all of our bread vanished, and the lad came again, to accuse me of the theft."

"What?" Her tired eyes stung. "What happened?"

"I kept my word and took the beating." He lifted his hand to thumb away the tear that slid down her cheek. "'Twas long ago, lass. Close your eyes now."

"I'm so sorry," she whispered, the words slurring as exhaustion swamped her. "I'll make it up to you, Cade. Promise…"

Lily fell into such a deep sleep that when Cadetrn shook her awake sometime later she felt entirely disoriented.

"Guard coming in," he whispered in her ear. "Secure our chains."

Lily winced as she pushed her power at the broken links to close them. Her head still throbbed miserably, although not as intensely as before. She looked up as Ochd trudged inside and bent to unlock her shackles. He eyed Cadeyrn and leaned over to tug on his chains before pulling her to her feet.

"Hendry wants you get food," Ochd told her as he gripped her arm and took her from the room.

Lily said nothing as she walked with him to the kitchen, where the druid stood ladling thick stew into two bowls.

"My thanks, Ochd," Hendry said. "I'll see to her now." He waited until the giant left. "I thought you and your new lover might appreciate a good meal."

From the smell of it he'd made it from mutton, mint and wild garlic, a combination that made her stomach turn. She also realized she'd neglected to put back on her ruined shoes, and knew without looking that dirt from the yard soiled her feet.

"You needn't have gone to the trouble. We're managing on the bread, cheese and water."

He added two oatcakes and some dried fruit to the tray. "A last meal should be special."

Lily wondered if he'd poisoned the stew. "Why the veiled threat? I've done everything you've asked of me."

"Do you ken where I'll find the Skaraven stronghold?" He straightened and set aside the pot and ladle, and watched her shake her head. "I suspected as much. You've been too busy facking the brute to question him. Or does he no' trust you?"

"We're getting on." She forced a sensual smile. "He does enjoy a good romp, I admit,

but these things take time. I should have the
location for you in another day or so."

"You'll have it by morning or I'll give the
Skaraven to my *caraidean*." Hendry picked up
the tray. "Aon has a rather grand notion for
the interrogation. 'Tis called quartering. He'll
bind the Skaraven's chains to four of the
horses and direct them to slowly pull his arms
and legs out of joint."

"That sounds unpleasant," she said,
feeling as if she might be sick now.

"If he doesnae answer our questions,
they'll be driven until they tear his limbs from
his body." He smiled gently. "How shall you
like facking an over-large stump?"

"I doubt he'll live long enough for me to
try," she told him, trying to sound bored. "But
all right, I'll convince him to tell me tonight."

"I hope you do, Sister. If we must kill the
Skaraven before he tells us where to find their
stronghold," he handed her the tray, "you'll
share his fate."

Hendry followed her back down the
passage to the storage room, where he opened
the door for her. When he locked her in, he
didn't leave, but hovered outside.

"We've real food tonight," Lily said briskly to Cadeyrn while shaking her head and shifting her gaze to the door. "I'll feed you first. You look hungry."

She sat down beside him, pointed to her ear and then at the shadows of Hendry's boots outside the door.

Cadeyrn nodded, his muscles coiling.

"You're not wanting the stew?" Lily said as she set the tray on the floor. "What am I going to do with you, you naughty lad? You need to eat if you're to keep up all these lovely muscles."

"Food isnae all I need," he told her as she straddled him.

Lily made sure to make as much noise on the bed as possible, but Hendry remained outside. "I can't believe you'd want me more than this delicious meal. Then again, you've been driving me mad ever since they brought you to me." She roughly tore at the collar of her tunic, and then pressed herself against his chest. "I know you want to touch me, lover, but you can't, not yet. You know what you have to do to be released."

"Take off your garments," Cadeyrn murmured. "I want to look upon you naked."

"Wicked lad," Lily said as she sat up to pull her tunic over her head and fling it to the floor. "What do you think of these?"

Cadeyrn uttered a low groan, all the while watching the door.

Lily continued the pantomime by shifting her weight to make the bed frame creak. "Oh, yes, kiss me again." She made a muffled sound as if his mouth covered hers, and saw his eyes shift to her face. Pretending they were making love had made her whole body heat up, and when she shifted back to rub her hands over his chest she felt the thick, hard length of his arousal pressing against her. "Are you ready for me, Cade? Do you want to be inside me?"

A glance at the door showed her that Hendry still listened, which made her swallow a shriek of frustration. Much more of this and she wouldn't have to act as if she were shagging the man.

Cadeyrn caught her gaze and nodded as if he knew what she was thinking.

"I can't help it," she said. "I'm already wet and ready for you." The truth spilled out of her as she bent her head to his, and pressed her lips to the corner of his mouth. "I need you."

"You have me, my lady," he murmured against her ear. "Take me as you will."

Lily had to climb off him to strip, which she did with shaking hands. By the time she got his trousers open his hands gripped the chains, and his chest heaved, but his eyes never left hers. When she hesitated, he nodded again.

Tears spilled from her eyes, but Lily dashed them away and smiled down at him. She imagined they were both somewhere far from here, alone in a lovely spot. A forest where everything was warm and green and quiet. Straddling Cadeyrn, she moved so that his swollen shaft pressed between her thighs.

He dragged in a breath as she reached down and curled her fingers around his cock. "My lovely, bold lass."

"I'll be whatever you like, Cade. You've only to say."

Wedging him against the hot, slick notch of her opening, she waited, her heart pounding. She couldn't bring herself to force him, not even with Hendry listening. He seemed to understand and arched his hips to work his straining cockhead into her softness.

"Take all of me, Lily," he said and truly sounded as if he were begging for it.

Was he?

Lily forgot about Hendry, his terrifying threats, and everything outside their room. Instead there was only Cadeyrn under her. Not even her limited experience mattered. She gave in to her senses as she slowly engulfed him, sinking down to impale her aching sex on his rigid length.

Nothing had ever felt as good as being stretched by his girth, which stiffened even harder once she had him in the silky clasp of her body. She tightened around him as her folds brushed his body hair, and then took him the rest of the way with one sweet, delicious push.

"Lily," he said, turning her name into a deep groan of pleasure. "Have me, aye. 'Tis good, so good."

She shook so hard that she had to brace her hands on his shoulders. That was when she saw the ink on his arm light up with a dark blue glow. It crept up the wall behind the bed as she moved on him, lifting and lowering herself, caressing him with every inch of her soaked, hot pussy. She couldn't take her eyes from it when she realized that it pulsed in time with his penetrations. The two seemed to be urging her on.

His head dropped back, and he went still as he saw the light. "My lady, wait."

All she could see was his golden eyes as the light shimmered over them both. "I can't," she gasped.

Something cool and soft glided over her shoulders and down her arms, as if he were stroking her with a huge fan made of feathers. But that couldn't be when his hands were still chained to the bed. The light rolled over them and sank into her, driving her to ride him as it took over her body.

"Dinnae fight it," he told her hoarsely, now yanking on the chains as he tried to free his wrists.

Lily breathed in the scent of him, dark and hot as a desert wind, and stopped resisting. She'd wanted this man since the moment she'd seen him riding after her, his burning eyes locked on hers. He'd had every reason to hurt her—she'd done nothing but lie to him from the start—and yet still he protected her.

What shall you give for my warrior? A thrumming voice demanded inside her mind.

My heart, Lily thought, stunned by how easily she answered. *My life.*

Remember that, Daughter, for I will.

The feathers on her arms turned to water, and slid down her skin in long, cool streams. Whatever was happening to them, it intensified every sensation for her. She bucked atop him, taking him into her very core. Over and over they came together, and faster and faster, until without warning she burst with cataclysmic ecstasy. Her body danced over his as he thrust deeper and harder.

Cadeyrn's muscles bulged as he arched under her, driving himself into her with one last, soul-shaking stroke before he groaned and began to jet.

She felt him flooding her and laughed with delight, for nothing felt as good as mingling her pleasure with his. Collapsing on him, her body still shivering with the delight he'd given her, she tucked her hot face against his neck.

Her headache had vanished, leaving her feeling only the sexy ache of satisfaction.

"Lily." He rubbed his chin over the top of her head, still panting as fast and hard as she was. "My battle spirit—"

"Shhh." She glanced at the light under the door, but the shadows of Hendry's boots had disappeared. That didn't mean they were safe from being overheard. Though the last thing she wanted to do was ever leave Cadeyrn again, she forced herself to get up. She went to the door and listened for a few moments before she came back to him. "I think he's gone, but keep your voice down." She saw how he was staring at her. "What's wrong?"

He peered at her. "Your arms."

"I'm all right." She rubbed them and felt a ghost of the tingling, caressing sensation. "They're a bit wet, is all. I've never sweated like that in my life." She smiled shyly at him. "But I liked it."

If anything, that made him tense even more. As he unhooked his wrist shackles from the chains, he said, "Come closer, please."

"Your ink made quite the light show. I had such a strange thing in my head while we were together, too," she said as she sat down beside him. "Like something was talking to me."

"Did it speak of me?" When she gave him a shocked look he closed his eyes. "Come lie with me." As soon as she stretched out beside him he murmured, "My battle spirit is the owl. 'Tis solitary, as I am. Yet it has marked you as mine." He traced his fingers over her shoulders and down along her outer arms.

The shapes he traced made her frown. "Marked my arms? No, those are only some gashes from the last time Coig beat me, and my jacket getting shredded by the portal."

"The wounds have gone, but there are scars now. Long and narrow, from here to here." He moved his hand from her elbow to her shoulder and back again. "Did you feel feathers on your skin?"

"Yes. I wondered how you did that." Her smile faltered. "But you didn't. You couldn't touch me."

"The owl did," he told her. "It saw and marked you. It healed you, but it put its wings on your arms."

Lily tried to peer at her skin. "It's odd, but I

don't mind being marked." Though she craned her neck, she couldn't get a good look. But the one thing she could see was that he was still upset. A thought occurred to her that made her go still. "Cade, whatever came of it, I'm not sorry. Are you? I thought you wanted it as much as I did."

"Aye," he declared in a husky voice. "And more."

His amber eyes gazed into hers with the same intensity she'd felt when she'd first seen him. A tiny shiver reminded her that she was still naked. As she gathered her clothes and dressed, he fastened his trousers.

"What did Hendry say to you?" he asked.

"He plans to give you to the guards in the morning to be tortured. Don't ask for the details, because they're ghastly." She sat down on the bed and gave a little push with her mind to release his ankle shackles. For the first time she didn't feel any pain from using her telekinesis. "We're out of time. We'll have to make a run for it tonight."

He nodded. "You should get the other lasses and take them through the portal." He sat up and and gently took hold of her hand, enveloping it completely with both of his. "I'll stay behind to hold off the *famhairean*."

"Are you mad?" Why was he talking like this? "You're going with us. We're taking you to your clan, and then…we'll go back to our time." Except now she hadn't the slightest desire to do so. In fact, just thinking about leaving Cadeyrn made everything inside her knot. "Let's talk about the diversion."

Chapter Nine

ONCE TWILIGHT FELL over the highlands, Bhaltair walked with Oriana from the village until they reached a quiet oak grove. The ring of carved stones protecting the portal glowed a cool white-silver as it sensed their druid blood.

"If you're weary, we may return and spend another night at the inn," he offered when her steps faltered. "'Tis no shame in tarrying if you arenae yet ready for the journey."

"I'm well, Master," Oriana said quickly. "The fever brew you made restored me entire."

His potion had paled before the resilience of her youth, Bhaltair thought, as he still silently wrestled with the soul-wrenching visions she had endured at the Wood Dream settlement. Once he'd nursed Oriana through the effects of her disastrous speak-seeing, however, she had regained her color and vivacity. He'd kept a close eye on her as she rode back with him to return the ponies they'd hired, but she showed no more signs of fever or fatigue. And yet the young acolyte still hesitated before entering the grove, and he saw doubt in her eyes.

"What gives you pause, Oriana?"

She turned to him, and her words came out in a rush. "Master, could you command the Watcher, the clan's shaman, to take us to the Skaraven? I could show their chieftain the torment of the Wood Dream."

"Why should you do that?" Bhaltair asked. "'Twas the cause of your seeing fever."

"I wasnae prepared the first time," she said and cast down her gaze, as was her custom when she felt fearful. "I ken myself strong enough now to do another speak-seeing. Surely such 'twould persuade Chieftain Brennus to our cause."

"Brennus would be as likely to pledge himself my slave." He watched her scowl and felt suddenly very old. "I ken you're eager to prove yourself, lass, but our past dealings with the clan havenae been kind nor wise. The chieftain wouldnae welcome us or our efforts."

"Then Brennus should be punished for his wickedness." Her innocent mouth took on a hard flatness as she regarded the portal. "I cannae help how I feel, Master. Had they fought the *famhairean* when you awakened them to immortality, we might have saved so many lives, my grandfather's included."

Her growing obsession with blaming the Skaraven for Gwyn's torture and death troubled Bhaltair, but the young druidess had lost to the giants her only blood-kin. It would require time and much caring for her, but in due course her anger would fade. He would see to it himself. He owed that much to his old friend.

"I willnae risk your health again so soon after a sickness, my dear one," Bhaltair advised as he took her hand, and gave it a reassuring squeeze. "Now come. I must attend to other matters, and assure that my tribe is safe among Ruadri's kin."

With a sigh Oriana nodded, and stepped

with him into the portal. A few moments later they gently landed on their feet in the north country, close to a roaring, white-watered river that surrounded a dark forest of towering, ancient trees.

"Stay close to me," Bhaltair advised her as they walked down the bank and stepped into what appeared to be roaring currents. "The channel of illusion narrows near the falls."

The river rushed around them as they walked across the concealed dry ground to the enormous shower of water spilling from a high cliff overhead. Bhaltair politely waited until the druid sentry guarding the falls opened a gap in the torrents.

Bhaltair leaned down to Oriana's ear. "If we encounter the Moss Dapple's headman while we're among them, dinnae mention the Watcher."

Oriana nodded, but clutched his arm as they walked into the pounding, splashing illusion and emerged on the other side surrounded by druids armed with axes.

Bhaltair had yet to grow accustomed to the isolated tribe's fierce defenders or their strange armor, which they wove from tight layers of tough, spiky vines. He still felt startled by their size as well. Most stood as tall and broad as mortal clan warriors. There had always been unsavory whispers about the tribe and why they never left their territory. In the past Bhaltair had paid them no heed, but now he wondered if some of what had been suspected was true.

Domnall, who oversaw the defense of the tribe's territory, came to greet him. As huge as the Skaraven's shaman, he carried an enormous axe that he held resting against his roof beam shoulder. His thorny chest plate creaked as he bowed without dropping his dark gaze.

"Come you now to seek sanctuary with your kin, Master Flen?"

"My acolyte and I wish but to visit the Dawn Fire, Domnall, that I may speak with some of our elders." He saw another defender move to join the overseer and pass a message scroll to him.

The big man glanced at the message before offering it to Bhaltair. "This came from the Skaraven."

Bhaltair bit back a mutter of impatience and took the scroll. Ruadri wrote in the old code they had used during his mortal life, which took Bhaltair a longer moment to decipher. As soon as he did he glanced at Oriana.

"My dear one, it seems I must speak to the headman directly." He regarded the overseer. "Would you be so kind as to escort my acolyte to my tribe, that she may take her rest with them?"

Domnall nodded curtly, but directed two of his men to usher Bhaltair to the Moss Dapple settlement.

Located deep within their enchanted forest, the tribe had built their homes and ritual buildings between and inside trees bespelled to grow wider than taller. Since the structures remained alive even after having been hollowed out, the tribe's homes sprouted vines, moss-draped branches, and twinned outgrowths of new trunks.

The Moss Dapple's headman occupied a taller, narrower home made of several birches that had been spell-melded together. He emerged as Bhaltair approached, tall and proud with his mane of white braids, his dark eyes sullen with the resentment of his interrupted hermitage. He looked past Bhaltair and made a waving gesture with one hand, and his escorts bowed and retreated.

"Come inside," Galan said in his sonorous voice, and once Bhaltair stepped into his abode shut the door and secured it. "You vowed you would no' seek me out."

"I'd hoped to leave you in peace, but events have persuaded me to intrude. I shall need every messenger bird you possess to send word to the other tribes. Since your overseer checks all messages, I must tell you first." He cleared his throat. "I shall ask them to watch for any sign of Cadeyrn, the Skaraven war master, or the quislings and their giants."

"What do you say?" Galan said in a raised voice and stared at him. "No. No' the Skaraven. Tell me you didnae awaken them from their graves."

Galan's expression made Bhaltair consider casting a protective body ward over himself, but he felt sure his old ally wouldn't attack him. Almost sure.

"The *famhairean* escaped the henge in the future and returned with the quislings to our time. The conclave agreed to awaken the

Skaraven to immortality, that they might again protect mortal and druid kind."

The headman closed his eyes. "You brought back Ruadri."

"I couldnae leave your son in the ground while awakening the rest of the clan." He rubbed his stiff knee. "He hasnae asked after you, Galan. Indeed, the one moment he mentioned you was to advise me to bring my tribe here for sanctuary. You never leave this settlement, so unless you send word to him your paths shall never cross."

Galan brought two cups to the table, and filled them with a strong-smelling, scarlet-colored liquid.

"We make this from pine. 'Twill burn a hole in your old belly."

The tall druid filled and drained his cup before adding more of the spirit.

Bhaltair had never known the big druid to take to drink. "'Tis no' a cause for reckless-ness, Brother."

With narrowed eyes the headman regarded him "Since Ruadri fell in battle I have never taken a mate, nor sired another bairn. Do you ken why?"

He felt the question like a thousand arrows pointed at his chest. "So that you might live in peace, and thoughtful contemplation, surely."

Galan laughed bitterly. "How polite you prattle. I cannae fack. No' since my love died whelping that monstrosity you call my son have I been capable. My cock remains as soft and useless as my life."

"I havenae taken a lover in many incarnations," Bhaltair admitted. "But I feel your pain."

"Do you indeed? Have you sired a son who tore apart his mother so badly that she bled to death in seconds after his birth? Did you watch it happen, and ken yourself useless to her? Did you listen to her final scream of agony? Does it haunt your dreams? Does it come back the moment you lay eyes on any wench?" Galan stared down into his cup, his eyes unfocused. "And you bring him back, this monster of my loins, and give him eternal life."

"Brother," Bhaltair said, reaching to touch Galan's twitching hand. "Ruadri didnae intend to kill his mother. A newborn can do naught but come into the world. 'Tis tragic that you lost her so cruelly, but the lad—"

"'Twas no' his birth or watching her die, you old stirrer. A mortal Pritani cannae reincarnate. I loved her more than my own life, and he saw to it that she shall never return to me. He took her from me forever." Galan met his gaze and Bhaltair startled when he saw something murderous. "You will bring Ruadri to me directly. As his sire I shall see to his future."

He couldn't fathom the vehemence in the headman's tone. "But you trained the lad, and taught him to keep watch for us."

The headman's lips stretched into a ghastly grin. "I did train him. I beat our ways into him, and burned my spells into his flesh, and caused him pain whenever I could. If he'd failed, I'd have happily sent him to the well of stars. Only he wouldnae. He's like a plague with no cure." All the emotion fled from Galan's expression. "Bring him to me. He may pay his debt to me by serving as my slave for eternity."

"I cannae," Bhaltair said gently. "The death of the two tribes freed the Skaraven from their indenture. He will never again wear the yoke of a slave." And now he understood why Ruadri felt such loathing toward his own people. "Galan, 'tis unlikely you should ever again lay eyes on your son. If you cannae forgive him, then you must forget this. Seek peace in what you have with your tribe."

"Peace, when I cannae sleep or think or *breathe* without memory of her." Without warning he took his cup and threw it into the hearth, making the fire flare up with a roar. "Get out of my sight."

Bhaltair quietly left and hobbled along the path to the back of the settlement, where his tribe now dwelled. They came from their new tree homes, greeting him with sober smiles veiling their relief. Bhaltair noted Domnall and his defenders watching them as he gathered with the elders and retreated into one of the hollowed dwellings.

"Brothers, I'm in dire need of your counsel," Bhaltair told them as they gathered chairs and sat in a circle. He related what he and Oriana had discovered at the Wood Dream settlement, and produced the cuff. "This ornament retains visions of their final day. Their end proved ugly and violent, but so did that of the Romans who murdered them."

"The invaders also died there?" one of the conclavists murmured.

"They became the *famhairean's* first victims. We didnae find bodies because they devoured their remains." He scanned the troubled faces around him. "That isnae the worst of it. The attack prevented the Wood Dream from completing their ritual that day. The magic remains unfinished and has tainted the land. No' a living creature goes near it. I think it must be part or all of what empowers the giants."

"'Twas tribal magic used for the ritual?" another elder asked, and when Bhaltair nodded he paled. "Then a member of the tribe must complete it."

Bhaltair sighed. "Of the Wood Dream bloodline, only Hendry Greum and Murdina Stroud remain."

That revelation caused the elders to begin talking all at once, each putting forth their opinions on how the quislings could be compelled to remove the taint. Bhaltair listened, but nothing they offered could be attempted with the giants still guarding the lovers. One by one the old druids fell silent, watching him as he turned the cuff in his hands.

"My thanks for your wisdom," Bhaltair said slowly. "I shall meditate on it. The other matter we must discuss is how long we Dawn Fire may abide with the Moss Dapple."

The elders exchanged telling glances but held their silence.

"Their headman is the newest incarnation of Galan," Bhaltair informed them. "He is the sire of Ruadri, our Skaraven Watcher." As the other druids reacted in shock he held up one hand. "'Tis no' that he despises his son. 'Tis how he governs this tribe. I ken that you have noticed the changes among the people here. The overseer, Domnall, and his men in partic- ular. To my eyes they resemble warriors, no' druids. I sense a strangeness about them as well. I believe Galan responsible for this, in some fashion. I would remain, and investigate, but I must go and meet with Ruadri in Aviemore."

The druid sitting beside him put his hand on Bhaltair's arm. "Do you reckon Galan has bred these defenders to be so, as you once did the Skaraven?"

"I cannae tell you yet. I dinnae ken if 'tis even my concern. But 'tis disturbing." He rubbed his eyes. "Any message sent from here shall be first read by Galan's overseer. You mustnae write or speak of this where your words shall meet unfriendly eyes or ears. We have taken sanctuary with the Moss Dapple. Until the lovers and their giants are defeated, the Dawn Fire must remain here in peace and gratitude."

Bhaltair ended the gathering by joining hands with the other druids and entreating the Gods to watch over their people. When he came out to seek a place of rest, Oriana stood patiently waiting for him.

"Master." She offered him her arm. "You must be hungry and tired."

"Never more so than tonight, my dear one." He tried not to lean on her too heavily. "Now, take me to the tribe's messaging place. I have many scrolls to write."

Chapter Ten

A S THE NIGHT deepened Cadeyrn waited at the door and listened for any sound to indicate the druids or their giants still roamed the mill house. He could hear only Lily's breathing, soft and quiet, and the scent of their ecstasy still lingering in the air. She had shown him delights he'd hardly imagined. He smiled a little at the memory of her finding her own bliss, and the wonder of knowing he could give that to her. The fact that Hendry had listened to them didn't trouble him. He was used to the tribe's shaman standing watch when he'd been with a pleasure lass.

Cadeyrn's smile faded. What gnawed at

him were the wings of scars now etched on Lily's arms.

He'd accepted his solitary state long before he and his clan had died. Since boyhood he'd always remained a little apart from his brothers. He'd even taken some pride in his reserve, for it gave him a sense of guardianship over the Skaraven. Never would he have to divide himself between care and duty. It had made him a canny warrior, and quickly elevated him to war master.

What he didn't know was how to be a mate. What was he to do with one chosen, not by him, but by the very spirit that had set him apart from his clan?

"Anything?" Lily whispered as she came to stand beside him.

He looked down at her. "I think they're all abed now." He saw the rags she'd torn earlier that now bound her feet. "You need boots."

Lily moved her shoulders. "I also need tea and biscuits, a jolly good soak in the tub, and a month in bed, boyo. Maybe two months."

Without thinking he moved to put his arm around her waist, and then let his hand fall. Since they'd made love, as she put it, he'd discovered that he could not be near Lily without wanting to touch her. She'd bespelled him with her lithe body and candid desires. If he wasn't careful he'd make himself her pleasure lad.

That he thought of having her again instead of escape made Cadeyrn wonder if she hadn't used some of her druid power on him. She might have pushed all the sense out of his brain. If he didn't dispel some of this wanting for her, he'd surely get them all killed.

"What I truly wish," Lily said, "is that Hendry had given us one more night together." She slipped her hand in his, weaving their fingers together. "Ready, then?"

"Aye."

Cadeyrn watched her face as she used her power to lift the bolt bar. When he felt the door shudder he opened it and stepped out into the passage. A quick look either way revealed no one to stop them. He kept hold of her as they went to the kitchen.

He hadn't misread the shift in her expression every time she used her talent, nor that it caused her headaches. She might have druid blood, but using the tree-knower powers caused her pain.

In an hour she shall never have to use them again, he told himself.

The diversion they had decided on depended much on the lamps and candles inside the mill. Cadeyrn took two watch lights and thrust their greasy ends into the bright embers still glowing in the hearth. When they flared, he handed one to Lily, who used hers to light every candle and lamp in the kitchen. Cadeyrn took kindling and dried moss from a covered bin near the hearth and portioned it in small mounds directly beside the candles and lamps. For the final touch Lily laid a trail of watch lights from the hearth across the floor and into all the passages, where Cadeyrn placed rags he smeared with butter. He took another moment to barricade all the entries before he rejoined her in the kitchen.

Lily led him out of the window and took him to the edge of the withered garden beyond it. There he saw the *famhairean* posi- tioned around the mill and granary, their eyes closed and their crackled faces still. Each held a club and a sword, which tempted Cadeyrn, but he wouldn't risk waking even one of them simply to arm himself.

Lily moved, and he followed her across the yard and behind the granary, where she looked out before she pulled him close and put her mouth on his.

Cadeyrn kissed her back, hard and fast, and then caught her face between his hands. "Burn it down, my lady," he murmured.

Lily's eyes turned black, and this time he felt the brush of something unseen and huge. It rushed away from them toward the mill. The muffled sound of things falling and crashing started. Soon smoke poured out of the windows, where orange-gold flames roared high.

The *famhairean* woke all at once, and when the nearest guards tried to enter the mill they found themselves locked out. Cadeyrn watched with Lily as they pounded on the doors and shouted for Hendry and Murdina. Lily made for the granary, but Cadeyrn held her back.

"No' yet," he told her in a low voice. He waited until the other giants rushed from the woods toward the mill. "Now."

They ran in opposite directions, Lily to the granary while he made for the wood shed behind the mill. On the wide wood door an iron latch was secured with a heavy lock. Cadeyrn cupped his hands at the door's edge.

"Perrin," he called quietly, trying not to draw attention. "Are you there?"

"Yes?" came a tremulous voice.

"Stand back from the door."

He called on his battle spirit and examined the entrance, but not the latch or the lock. His attention was immediately drawn to its tired hinges. Though sturdy nails held them to the shed, they were but nails. He backed up two paces, seeing the weakest ones as though from up close. A blow to the door planks, in just the right spot, would cause them to wrench free from the wood. He lowered his shoulder and ran. Splinters flew and metal squealed as the door broke free of its top hinge. Cadeyrn's momentum carried him through the entry, his boots snapping the wood around the bottom hinge. The remainder of the door swung wildly by only the useless latch and lock.

A thin, young lass with eyes like a frightened doe stood trembling in the corner.

"I am Cadeyrn," he said and held out his hand. "Lily sent me. We must hurry."

Though she slowly extended her hand, he didn't wait for her to cross the room. In two steps he'd swept her up in his arms and sprinted for the granary. The millstone was laying on the ground and Lily emerged with two other women.

"*Perrin*," said the dark, sturdy one, as they all hid behind the granary.

"Ro," the thin lass said as Cadeyrn set her down. Though the two embraced, Cadeyrn saw that it was more that the taller one supported Perrin, lest she fall.

"This is Perrin's sister Rowan," Lily said. "And Emeline."

Emeline regarded Cadeyrn. "Thank you for helping us."

"Quit chatting with the hot guy, Florence," Rowan said, her voice tired. She knelt in front of her unsteady sister to take her on her back. As she stood, she circled Perrin's thighs around her waist and gripped them from the bottom. "We need to blow this place right now." Her speckled eyes shifted to Cadeyrn. "Are you our hero? Never mind. Let's get to the portal."

Cadeyrn tried to take her burden from her, but she shrugged him off and took off at a trot. He nodded, but when he saw Emeline was falling behind he snatched the nurse up in his arms.

"Hold onto my neck, my lady."

Her crystalline eyes glowed brightly blue as she smiled up at him. "You're my hero, lad."

When they reached the oak grove, Lily came to an abrupt stop, and as Cadeyrn set down the nurse he saw why. A mountain of millstones had been piled in the center of the grove, completely covering the portal.

Lily swiped at her ear as she marched up to the stones, and focused on them before she closed her eyes. The heavy rock wheels shook, some dislodging to slide a few inches, but none of them moved.

Falling to her knees, Lily clutched her head, and then gave him a desperate look. "I can't budge them. It's like they're glued together to the ground."

"Hendry was out here today with Aon and Dha," Rowan said. "They must have blocked it with the stones and used his mojo to seal it off." She looked back toward the mill. "We can't go back there and pretend like nothing happened. We've got to run."

"No," Lily insisted. She trembled as she stood and dragged in a deep breath. "I have this."

Before anyone could stop her Lily's eyes blackened as she used her power on the stones, which rumbled before blasting out a wave of their own dark power.

"*Lily*," Cadeyrn yelled and ran to her. He caught her as she crumpled and went limp.

"Let me see her," Emeline said.

She touched her fingertips under Lily's jaw and drew them back wet and red. She tilted the unconscious woman's head to the side, revealing a thin trickle of blood inching down from her ear.

"Gods above," Cadeyrn muttered as his gut clenched. "Her power makes her bleed?"

"Aye, sometimes from the nose. Never from the ear until now. Lily." The nurse repeated her name several times as she gently pushed up her eyelids and peered at her darkened eyes. "I dinnae ken how badly she's hurt, but she'll likely be unconscious for a time."

"We are out of time," Rowan said. She adjusted her sister on her back. "Cade, right? We need to get the hell away from here, right now."

He lifted Lily in his arms and surveyed the horizon beyond the forest. "I need water—a loch, a river, even a stream will do."

"There aren't any lakes for miles," Rowan told him. "Ochd told me that they dammed the one stream that was close at its source in the hills. I think it's why Hendry chose this place—so you guys couldn't use the water to get at him and Murdina."

His jaw tightened, and he looked to the east and north. If he'd been with his brothers they could run for hours until they reached safety. Even if they could rouse Lily and Perrin, four battered, starved lasses would never keep up with him. "Then we're for the hills. Follow me."

Cadeyrn held Lily close while they made their way through the trees. Deliberately avoiding the old farm trails, he led them in a scattered pattern that would help confuse any giant that picked up their trail. He also left passage markers only another Skaraven would recognize, so that if by chance the clan tracked them to the mill they would know where he'd taken the lasses.

Rowan proved to be as strong as she looked, and even carrying her sister kept pace with him. Emeline had to trot to do the same, and quickly grew breathless, but did not complain. Cadeyrn couldn't carry two women to safety with any speed, so he stopped at the edge of the woods.

"We'll rest here," he said.

"Thank you from the bottom of my feet," Emeline gasped but didn't sit down. Instead she came to look at his lady. "Has she opened her eyes yet?"

"No, my lady." He brushed a lock of pale hair back from her brow. "She's no' even stirred."

Rowan knelt beside them to gently place her sister on her back. Perrin was unconscious.

"Em, would you mind having a look at Perr after you finish with Lily?"

The nurse nodded, and once she'd checked his lady's neck, eyes and ears she went to Perrin. "Good pulse," she told Rowan, and carefully felt along the thin lass's arms and legs. "No new injuries. Do you ken if she's eaten anything?"

"Knowing my big sis, probably not," Rowan said, sounding deeply annoyed.

Cadeyrn saw Perrin's eyes open and turn opaque as she stared at him.

"Take us before the snow, War Master." Her voice sounded as if it came over a long distance.

"You're a master of war?" Rowan said, gaping at him.

"Aye, for my clan," Cadeyrn answered though he kept his gaze on the sister.

Lily had told him that Perrin could see the future. Her lashes fluttered, her eyes cleared, and she peered up at her sister.

"Hey," she said. "We're not at the mill."

"I should have left you there," Rowan said as she hugged her sister. "We're almost home, Perr. Just stay awake for a while, okay?"

Cadeyrn let the lasses rest as long as he dared while he gathered stones and embedded them in the soil in a particular pattern beneath his final passage marker. When he finished the message he checked the sky.

Heavy clouds approached from over the treetops.

Before the snow, Perrin had said.

Cadeyrn eyed the incoming storm. He had always relied on his own senses rather than take direction from the Gods, let alone the magic folk. But there was no doubt the temperature was dropping. As the wind grew biting, Emeline huddled close to the sisters. The snow would be here within the hour.

He scanned the opposite direction. There were hills beyond the forest. He used his gift to examine the strange rocky slopes in one particular section. A deep, wide fracture ran from its base to its peak. The crevasse divided it almost perfectly into two hills. Though a natural formation, it could offer a high ground advantage and admirable protection.

Before the snow.

They would flee in the direction of the storm, not before it reached them.

"We'll cross the far side of the fields, and circle back to there," he told the ladies, and pointed to the base of the fissure. "Likely we'll find a cranny or cave where we might shelter from the storm."

"And move on tonight, as soon as we can," Rowan said, glancing at her sister. "I don't suppose anyone brought any food or water flasks?"

"We'll have snow to melt for water," Emeline assured her. "If we spot anything edible on the way, we'll gather it."

"Since Lily's still conked out, and I don't know an endive from poison ivy, you're our spotter," the dark lass told the nurse. "Perr, you ready to take a hike?"

The thin lady nodded, and with her sister's help got to her feet.

"If you tire, tell me," Cadeyrn advised her. "We'll rest where 'tis safe."

"That's nowhere around here," she said. Though she swayed for a moment, she squared her shoulders. "Come on, let's go."

Crossing the dry cobbles of the river bed had been tricky and slow, and the trek took longer than Cadeyrn had estimated. By the time they reached the base of the divided hills Perrin had gone gray and trembling. Emeline's face looked as white as the snow that had begun falling on their heads. Rowan had her arms around both women to support them.

She tilted her head back to look up at the fissure and frowned.

"What's that?" she asked, and nodded at a series of jagged stone shelves inside the huge crack.

Cadeyrn carried Lily with him as he drew closer and felt a surge of satisfaction. "Stairs." Quickly he put his lady down behind some brush, and gestured for the other lasses to join her. "I'll scout it first. Stay here and watch for them."

An icy wind buffeted Cadeyrn as he climbed to the lowest rock shelf and inspected the sloping sides around him as he ascended. He saw no chisel or hammer marks on the moss-splotched stone, but someone long ago had excavated the interior and fashioned the stairs. He followed them up to an arch carved with Roman letters on either side. Beyond the entry stood the ruins of a fortlet within a brick enclosure.

He'd seen several of the same sort during his mortal life, when the invaders had flooded into Caledonia. This had once been a Roman garrison post. It had been built so deeply inside the crevasse it could not be seen from the outside of the divided hills.

Hurrying back down to the ladies, Cadeyrn silently thanked his battle spirit. "There is shelter for us."

This time when Cadeyrn lifted Lily into his arms she stirred and huddled closer to his chest. A second wave of relief flooded him as he led the other women into the crevasse.

"Mind your footing," he warned them. "'Twill be easy to slip on the steps."

He had them climb up in front of him, and when they reached the arch, they beheld the ancient fortlet with wide eyes.

"Whoa," Rowan murmured as she went to touch the chiseled letters. "This looks like Latin. The ancient variety."

"It says 'The Ninth Legion, sentry post, commanded by Quintus Seneca,'" Emeline said, translating the Roman words. "'The eyes of Rome never close.' Ancient, too, the date is from the first century."

"I'm pretty sure their eyes are closed now," Rowan told her. "We need to get out of this snow and wind, Cade."

He nodded, and carried Lily through the

arch and into the fortlet. Tracks worn into the stone led him to a section of mortared rock that appeared to be cracked in two places, when he pushed on it the wall swung inward to reveal a threshold of rotted wood.

"Good thing they made use of the hill for most of their structures." Rowan nodded toward the sagging remains of a watch tower made of rotted logs. "Stay away from that unless you want it to collapse on your head."

The interior of the fortlet had been divided into three sections of excavated rock, all of which had already filled with snow. Cadeyrn spotted rings where large canvas tents had once been tied, and a huge fire pit still filled with gray ash and blackened bones. He carried Lily over to the only fully-enclosed structure still standing: a large stone-walled storage building built into the side of the crevasse. An outcropping had formed the roof, and a rack of rusted iron barred the two entries.

"Allow me," Rowan said and took hold of the crumbling iron. She yanked it out with a single tug. Orange-red flakes drifted around her feet as she set the rack to one side and peered in. "Some old shields and plenty of rat nests, but no Romans." Rowan nodded toward the interior and held out her arms for Lily.

Cadeyrn carefully handed her over before he ducked through the entry. Rows of rusted rectangular shields had been left stacked against the walls. What he thought had once been sacks of grain appeared to have been used by vermin as nests until the sacking turned to dust. Spiderwebs canopied a mass of crocks and urns, some cracked and crumbled.

He returned to the ladies and took Lily from Rowan. "'Tis sound enough to spend a night, and 'twill keep us out of the cold."

"Can we risk a small fire?" Emeline asked.

During their flight, Cadeyrn had noted the terrain, possible escape routes, and also the way the storm had chased them.

"This wind should whisk away the smoke," he said and nodded.

Emeline sighed with relief. "Rowan, would you collect some dry wood? I'd rather no' burn that sacking. Perrin, come and share your heat with Lily until we have it going."

Cadeyrn was impressed by how quickly

and calmly the nurse took charge of their care. Once he lay Lily down beside Perrin in the warmest corner, he covered them both with his tartan.

Lily's eyes fluttered again, and this time she opened them to slits. "Safe?"

"Aye," he said and felt no shame in lying to her.

When she closed her eyes, he looked at the seam of dried blood that ran down the side of her throat. In his memory he saw how weak she'd been when she'd returned from the granary. Despite knowing what it'd do to her, and without a word of complaint, Lily had tried to move the stones that covered the portal. Had it been a mountain, Cadeyrn knew the brave lass would have tried that too.

In that moment something that had wrapped cold and tight around his heart melted away.

Perrin shifted her so that Lily's head rested against her shoulder. "I'll look after her, Cade."

He hated to leave her, but the rest of the fortlet needed to be checked. He also had to find something for the lasses to eat, or they wouldn't have the strength to push on at nightfall.

"We'll be very well," Emeline said, startling him as she took a rock and struck it against the edge of a rusted shield, nodding with satisfaction when it produced a spark. "Go on with you. I'll no' leave them alone."

Outside the storage building Cadeyrn encountered Rowan carrying a bundle of twigs and branches under one arm, and a shield heaped with clean snow.

"Wait here for a minute," she told him, and disappeared into the storage building to return without the wood or snow. "I think I found some food, but I need your help to reach it."

Cadeyrn considered telling her any food the Romans had left behind would be dust, but followed her over to a stunted tree that had grown in the unlikeliest of places.

"This must have been their latrine." She nodded at a short row of broken slates with privy holes cut through them. She patted the tree, which had grown up out of a seam in the rock. The way she studied the trunk and limbs said she saw more in the wood than met his eye. "See that hole that's gnawed around the edges?" She pointed to a hollow about half way up the trunk. "How much you want to bet that's a squirrel stash?"

Cadeyrn hefted himself up to peer inside. He reached in, retrieved a handful of big nuts, and tossed one down to her.

"Chestnuts," she said, chuckling as she kissed it. "I love it when I'm right. Let me get something to put them in." She hurried off.

Finding a more comfortable spot to wedge himself, Cadeyrn surveyed the surrounding structures. The fortlet seemed too small to be a proper Roman post, and the Romans had gone to great lengths to conceal it. More likely they built it as a lookout for a small detachment of men. Since it remained intact no one else had ever found it, either.

Assessing the fortlet didn't keep Cadeyrn's gaze from shifting back to the stone building. Although he knew they needed the food, and he had yet to check the rest of the post, he wanted to go in and take Lily from Perrin. His arms ached to hold her until she woke again. Cadeyrn had always prided himself on being immune to the weaknesses of other men. Lily, it seemed, had turned him into a lovesick lad.

"Hey, Master of War." Rowan appeared at the base of the tree and held up a large old ewer. "Let's play catch."

Chapter Eleven

✦✦✦

AS THE FIRE consuming the mill roared, Hendry wrapped a blanket around Murdina's slumped shoulders. Much of her silvered red hair had been singed, and soot blackened her nose and mouth.

"We might have died," the druidess whispered, watching the black smoke rolling out to engulf the sagging roof. "That sly bitch and her cursed lover set fire to our home."

"'Twas only a place we used," he chided gently. "When I build you our home, goddess mine, it shall be a castle. You shall rule as Queen of the new world we make."

"We could take the *caraidean* and run away," she looked up at him, tears flooding her reddened eyes. "We could live in the land of the white bear, where humans cannae. The sun doesnae set there for two seasons. They could never hurt us again."

"You would never be warm again." And the isolation and cold would likely drive her completely mad, although Hendry couldn't say that much. "Murdina mine, my dearest, truest love, you mustnae surrender to fear. Soon all humans shall be naught more than the dust beneath our feet. We shall prevail over them and show the Gods that this world can be paradise."

"You will give Lily to me when we find them?" she asked, sobbing the words. "I want to burn her hair off. I want her to choke and wheeze and scream as I do. Please, Hendry."

"She shall be yours to punish," he lied to her.

Keeping Murdina pressed against him as she wept, he watched Aon and the other giants drag out the last of the *famhairean* who had burned to save him and his lover. A third of their *caraidean* had been reduced to charred stumps. He'd taken the precaution of having some new forms made for their souls to inhabit, but not nearly enough.

He felt Murdina shudder violently, and then she pushed away from him and ran to the granary. Before he could go after her Ochd came to him, his refined face smudged and his eyes filled with hurt.

"Rowan took her sister," the *famhair* told him, and handed him a small etched rune that Hendry had weeks ago slipped into the dancer's pocket. "I found this with her clothes in the granary. How long before she sheds the effects of your magic?"

"Too soon." To control both sisters, Hendry had placed the charm on Perrin to induce weakness by stifling her appetite. He cursed himself for forgetting about it when he'd given them all clean clothes to wear. "'Twill be easy enough to replace once we take them back from the Skaraven."

Aon and Coig joined them. "Twenty-one burned. We've but seven forms prepared."

"Leave your brothers to me," Hendry said. "I shall restore them. You must track the Skaraven and our sisters."

The leader of the giants scanned the horizon. "We cannae release volatiles in this storm. They willnae travel hence or back to us."

"Then use their logic to track them," the druid advised. "To find sanctuary among mortals, they should have gone south or east. Yet the Skaraven can be canny. Cadeyrn would have taken them north, into the hills, or west, to the midlands."

"'Twould be foolish to walk the females with the storm," Aon said. "They wouldnae go far before succumbing to the cold. We should track west, away from it."

Hendry had learned to trust the giants' instincts. "Agreed. When you find them, dinnae kill any of the females but Lily Stover. Make it look as if she fought you."

Coig gave him a splintered grin. "I shall see to it, Wood Dream."

"What of the Skaraven?" Ochd asked.

"Do as you wish," Hendry said. "But bring back his head to me. I'll mount it on a pike for Murdina."

Once the giants trudged off he went to the granary and looked inside. Murdina had torn the place apart, destroying everything left behind by the women. She sat in a pile of grain now, holding a handful and letting it trickle through her fingers.

"Like the stones by the loch," she murmured as she looked up. "Do you remember that time I picked them up and put them in my pockets, my love?"

He sat down beside her and guided her head to rest against his shoulder. "How could I forget the most wondrous night I've ever known?"

It might have been twelve centuries past, but it was the only time from his mortal life that he cared to remember. In every incarnation Hendry had always been ruled by the bond between his deepest emotions and his ability, a razing force that was rare even among the most powerful druid tribes. During his last life his father had taught him to control it through prayer and calming rituals. He had also taken long swims in the cold, dark waters of Loch Ness.

"You mustnae indulge yourself, my son," Angas Greum advised him. "Denying your urges shall wither them. Apply yourself to that end, and in time you shall rid yourself of them. 'Tis the only manner in which you shall walk the path of the righteous."

Hendry had tried to do as his father asked. By the time of his initiation he had grown detached and aloof, but the clear path to right-eousness had never been shown to him. His power simmered inside him, a sleeping monster. He'd even considered leaving the tribe and isolating himself away from those he might harm.

After a disagreement with their headman one night had pushed his temper to dangerous heights, Hendry had gone to the loch. Instead of stripping out of his robes and wading into the water, he'd begun gathering stones.

A shadow flitted out of the trees and came to join him. "What do you here, Hendry Greum?"

He eyed his young cousin. Since birth she had never quite been of a right mind. Some thought her mad, while others thought her touched by the Gods. Either way, the tribe avoided her almost as much as they did him.

"I told you no' to follow me about anymore, Murdina Stroud."

"I forgot." She held out a smooth stone to

him. "Do you build a cairn? Do you wish me to help?"

"I mean to drown myself," he heard himself blurt out. He shoved the stones in his pockets and forced out a bitter laugh. "I but jest with you. Go home, lass."

"Home to my mother, who hates me, and my father, who says I must mate with that fat slug Dirkus?" She shoved the stone in her pocket. "I'd rather drown myself with you."

Hendry knew the young druidess to be unhappy, but the calmness with which she spoke of ending her life touched his cold heart. It also sickened him to think of her mated to Dirkus, who ever stank of the manure he collected for the food gardens.

"Your mother envies your beauty and power. She has neither, you ken." When she shrugged he added, "Your father cannae force you to mate with anyone. Go and speak to the headman. He shall tell you the same."

Murdina gathered more stones. "If I cannae be with you, Hendry, I dinnae wish to live."

Hendry watched her fill her pockets until they bulged. Convinced her threat was only for his benefit, he didn't move as she waded out into the water. She strode forward without a pause and was soon up to her waist. In moments the water covered her chest. Something in the set of her shoulders told him this was no' play. But surely she didn't intend to end herself just because he was.

As the loch lapped at her chin, she glanced back at him. Now she would call for his help, surely. He couldn't stand by and watch her drown, of course, but he'd let her get a good dunking before he pulled her out.

"I love you," Murdina called to him. "I'll await you in the well."

She sank out of sight, rippling the water.

Hendry waited for her to stand and end the ruse, but the seconds ticked by as he watched the placid surface. Suddenly bubbles burst through, but of Murdina there was no sign. He ran to the loch, diving in and swimming frantically until he found her. Even with the stones weighing her down she felt like a small bairn in his arms. He dragged her to the shore, where he blew his breath into her mouth until she coughed up the water she'd swallowed. He turned her on her side and held her until she could breathe freely once more.

"You mad little wench," he said, pushing the wet hair back from her pale face. Tenderly he cradled her on his lap. "You ken 'tis forbidden for us to love. We're blood-kin."

"I dinnae care. I cannae sleep or eat for thinking of you." She caught his hand and brought it to her lips. "Come with me to the well, please, Hendry. Only there can we be together."

He saw in her eyes the same wretchedness that dwelled in him, and that finally undid him. He pulled her close and kissed her wet mouth until she gasped with delight. Then he carried her to a mossy spot beneath the trees and took her maidenhood, as passionately as if they'd just been mated. That illicit act brought him the only joy he had ever known —and it had sealed their fate.

They could not reveal to the tribe that they had become lovers—his mother and hers were sisters by blood—but they defied druid law and met in secret whenever they could. Murdina used her talents with herbs to make a potion to keep from conceiving, and

concocted soothing draughts to help Hendry
control his temper. In front of others they
remained polite cousins, and their act proved
so effective no one ever questioned it.
Murdina refused to mate with anyone, as did
Hendry, but few offered. In time their parents
died, and at last they were able to live together.
The tribe even approved. The headman
thought it kind of Hendry to provide home
and hearth for his spinster cousin.

How they had laughed about the tribe's
ignorance as they made love every night in
Hendry's bed. They began to make plans to
leave the settlement and live away from druid
kind, where mortals would think them only a
middle-aged man and his wife.

"I shall love you forever," Murdina would
tell him. "Naught can ever come between us."

Naught had, until the Romans attacked
the Wood Dream in the midst of their solstice
ritual. If he and Murdina had not slipped
away to make love, they would have died
along with their tribe that day. Returning to
find their slaughtered kin scattered across the
glen had been as shocking as discovering the
tribe's wooden guardians had come to life.

"I dinnae fathom this," Murdina had said, clinging to his arm. "Why did the Gods spare us?"

Hendry gazed down at the tiny corpses of two bairns barely weaned. Beyond them the hulking giants gouged at the ground, digging graves to bury the dead. "To make right a terrible wrong." His power surged inside him. "The Gods shall show us the path."

So they had, until Bhaltair Flen had stopped them.

In the quiet of the granary a sudden desperation seized Hendry, and he pulled Murdina into his arms.

"I willnae permit him to take you from me."

He pressed her back into the grain, dragging up her night gown and jerking open his trews. As soon as Murdina felt him hard against her she clamped her thighs around his hips and urged him inside her.

Being buried deep in her quim brought to Hendry the only peace he had ever known. Moving steadily inside her, he looked into her eyes and watched the fear fade into hunger for him.

"Never shall I let you go from me again, sweeting mine," he said, groaning the words as she shivered beneath him. "You belong to me, body and soul. You remember that, Murdina. You cling to that, and naught shall part us."

Their coupling grew rough and wild, and when they both shuddered to climax Hendry felt his own strength and purpose renewed. Gods, how much he loved this woman, and now it would be forever more. He'd have her every hour if she needed that to remind her.

"I need only you beside me," Murdina whispered, making him realize he'd given voice to his thoughts. "But take me again, Hendry. Take me until I beg you stop."

"Then 'twill be for eternity," he told her, and kissed the delighted smile on her lips.

Chapter Twelve

LILY WATCHED CADEYRN add some wood to the brazier Emeline had fashioned from an old shield and some rocks. She still felt a little thick-headed from whatever had knocked her out cold at the portal, but it was fading. She still couldn't believe Emeline's claim that the Skaraven warrior had carried her for miles. But then there was the way he kept glancing at her —as if all Cadeyrn wanted was to get her alone and put his hands on her.

She wanted that too. Just his glances made her whole body heat from the inside.

"If we had some hot chocolate," Rowan said as she used a stick to fish more of the roasted chestnuts from the brazier's hot ashes,

"and a turkey in the oven and some holiday
tunes playing, this would be perfect."

"We've naught but very cold water,"
Emeline advised her as she checked the inside
of another stone dish before dipping it in the
shield of slushy snow. "Cade, come and have
some before Perrin gobbles the lot."

The dancer stopped cramming the roasted
nut meats in her mouth to glare at the nurse.

"I haven't eaten for weeks, thank you very
much." She finished chewing and swallowed,
sighing blissfully. "Oh, but they do taste
wonderful, don't they?"

Cadeyrn crouched beside Lily to survey
the remaining nuts. She peeled one of the
cooled dark brown husks from her portion and
offered him the wrinkly, pale nut.

"Here. I'm full."

He took it from her fingers with his mouth,
his lips brushing against her skin in a kiss only
she saw and felt. "My thanks."

Since they'd come here everything he said
to Lily sounded like an invitation to shag.
Then again, every time she looked at him she
was imagining him naked.

"The water doesn't taste anything like

Christmas," Rowan said, wrinkling her nose after taking a sip. "More like old rusty Roman shield."

"We could all use a wee bit of iron to build our blood," Emeline said and then stood. She took in a quick breath and turned away from everyone. "Rowan, watch the fire. I need some air. Excuse me."

Lily caught a glimpse of the blush darkening Emeline's cheeks before she stepped outside. The nurse had picked up on someone's emotions, and they'd embarrassed her. Rowan and Perrin seemed happier than she'd ever seen them, so that left her and Cadeyrn.

Gazing up into the warrior's golden eyes, she saw the same yearning hunger that she felt. It made her beyond happy to have gotten the other women away from the druids, but now all she wanted was her Skaraven warrior and a nice, quiet, private spot.

Cadeyrn looked from her to where Emeline stood outside and back again. Lily trailed her fingertips over her lips, still faintly swollen from his kisses, and saw his mouth curve. Then she stroked her hand along her arm, and saw his smile fade as his eyes turned a hot bronze.

"I can't believe how hungry I am," Perrin said as she tossed some husks into the flames and reached for more. "It's like I haven't eaten for weeks."

"You haven't," Lily reminded her, feeling a little breathless. "Not that we had anything scrumptious to nibble on, but you barely touched a morsel."

"You ate like a pig yesterday morning, too," Rowan said, and gave her sister a measuring look. "Right after you changed into that dress."

The dancer nodded. "I remember. As soon as I got out of my clothes my stomach started growling like crazy."

Lily glanced at Cadeyrn, who was frowning now. "Did Hendry or Murdina do something to make her hungry?"

"If they did, I reckon 'twas the opposite, my lady," he said slowly. "They might have bespelled her to no' want food, mayhap to keep her weak."

"If they did, then why didn't they hex the rest of us?" Rowan asked.

"To control you," Lily said before Cadeyrn could reply. "You're the strongest and, I'll wager, the least fearful."

"Aye, and you've had more chances to escape than any of us," Emeline said as she rejoined them. "Ochd took you out to the woods alone just the other day. Why didn't you make a try for the portal?"

"I thought about it, but I couldn't." The carpenter suddenly looked uneasy. "I couldn't leave behind my sister. I swore to Marion before she died—the woman who adopted us —that I'd always watch over Perr."

Perrin stared aghast at her. "Mother made you promise that? But why?"

"I don't know. Maybe because you're totally clueless. Nothing bad ever happened to you before we got dragged through the oak time tunnel." Rowan spread her hands. "What was I supposed to do? The old hag was dying. She'd have come back to haunt me."

They all knew the carpenter to be utterly devoted to her sister, but what she said made no sense to Lily. "Touching, but you might have used the portal to go for help and come back for us."

"You wouldnae go, Lady Rowan, or you couldnae?" Cadeyrn asked her.

"It's just Rowan, and I couldn't go." She sounded confused now. "I've wanted to. Even before we got here I thought about going off on my own plenty of times. Then I'd hear Marion in my head, and remember making the promise, and I'd forget about it."

"But you never said a word to me," Perrin said, her eyes wide.

Rowan shrugged. "No point."

"Well, that's not happening anymore," Perrin said firmly. "I don't need a caretaker, and Marion had no right to ask that of you. When we get back home, it stops. You get on with your life and do what you want with it."

"Sure," Rowan said smothering a yawn. "I don't know about the rest of you, but I could use some sleep. Cade, can we curl up around the fire? The embers should keep us warm until morning."

That put an end to the strange discussion. Cadeyrn gouged out four hollows in the dirt floor, and filled them with fresh pine needles and dried leaves he collected from outside. He then tore his tartan into four pieces and covered the mounds, making them into surprisingly comfortable makeshift beds.

"I'll stand watch while you sleep," he told them.

Once he'd left, Rowan curled up beside her sister and watched the fire die down until her eyes closed. Emeline used some of the melt water to wash her hands and face before she offered the last of it to Lily. She also tore one of her rags into strips and knelt down to tie Lily's shoes back together.

"When we reach the Skaraven we'll ask to borrow some shoes for you," Emeline said. "These need to be tossed in the rubbish."

"You know about me and Cade shagging, don't you?" Lily asked as she tidied up. "And you know what he feels for me, too."

"Oh, aye." The nurse stifled a laugh. "He's what you Brits call completely besotted." Her expression sobered. "You've no' told him about what Coig did to you."

Lily endured a wave of nausea before she shook her head. "I didn't know you could read minds."

"I cannae. But I'm a nurse, and I saw the state you were in when that bastart carried you

to the portal in our time." Emeline's mouth
tightened as she knotted the last rag strip. "I'm
no' one to give advice—I've never had a
romance—but he should know what will
happen to you here…and before you came."

"You can know all that from your power?"
Lily asked, startled.

"Some of it." She grimaced. "I ken it's
none of my business."

"I think we're long past pretending to be
polite strangers." Lily smiled a little. "If
Hendry was telling the truth, which he almost
never does, and we get away safely, the Skaraven will return us to the future. Well, you lot
anyway. I may end up in a dungeon for
snatching Cade."

"Talk to him, Lily," the nurse said. "He
deserves to ken the full truth." She offered her
a sympathetic smile before she lay down and
closed her eyes.

Lily felt tempted to retreat back into
herself and tell Cadeyrn nothing. So, they'd
shagged. That didn't give him a front row seat
to the story of her life, and what had been
done after she'd been ripped from it. All he'd

done was go along with her little ruse to fool Hendry—

You keep yourself emotionally numb as a defense, her therapist had told her. *If you convince yourself that you don't feel anything for anyone, then they can't hurt you.*

She didn't feel numb anymore. Cadeyrn had gotten to her, unlocked a part of her that she hadn't known still existed. She knew exactly when he had opened her heart, too: when he'd told her about the beating he'd taken for protecting a starving boy. He'd put his trust in that boy, and her, and had suffered because of it. He still didn't understand why she'd done it. She wanted him to know that, to know who she was.

It would take every ounce of her courage to trust him with all of her dark secrets. But if anyone could ever understand her, Cadeyrn was her man.

Lily left the other women sleeping and wrapped herself in the torn length of tartan before she ventured outside. She felt a little as if she were walking toward the edge of a cliff. The storm had dropped a prodigious amount of snow on the hills and inside the crevasse, but the sky looked clear.

When Lily reached the arch, she found the alcoves empty, only to jump as Cadeyrn leapt up from the steps leading down from the fortlet.

He immediately came to her and put his hands on her shoulders. "Trouble?"

"No," she said, trying to smile and failing miserably. "What were you doing down there?"

"Leaving a message for my brothers, that they might ken where we shall go on the morrow." Cadeyrn studied her face for a moment, and then drew her inside the alcove out of the wind. "You should be sleeping."

"Says the man who's been awake for God only knows. I need to talk to you about something...private." She took off the tartan, shaking the snow from it before she spread it over the stone bench. "Would you sit with me?"

"If I may?" When she smiled he lifted her in his arms and placed her on his thighs. "'Twill be warmer for us both."

Being close to him made her arms tingle with something she'd never before felt.

"You do keep me cozy."

"You've no' often been so," Cadeyrn guessed.

"No." Lily wasn't sure how to begin, and then the words simply poured out of her. "My father was quite wealthy and important. He was a big man, very tall and heavy, and stupendously strong, too. He expected everything to be exactly as he wished. When it wasn't, he'd get angry, and that was often. Sometimes daily." She felt sick, and paused until the sensation passed. "My father bullied and terrified me all of my life. I can't remember a time when I wasn't afraid of him." She stared out at the fallen snow. "He also beat my mother for twenty-one years, until she killed herself. After she died he started hitting me."

"Bastart," Cadeyrn muttered under his breath.

"Yes, he was." She cleared her throat. "He was quite careful to keep anyone from finding out what he did to us. He told my mother that he'd kill us both if she told anyone—in front of me. I was five years old, and I still remember her expression. She believed him, and so did I."

Lily told him how her father deceived everyone, even their servants, into believing he was a kind and generous man. How in private he would take out his frustrations on her mother, who gradually became more depressed and fearful. How he began keeping Lily from her mother in order to have more control over them both. How it felt to grow up in a house where even the slightest mistake could result in a terrible punishment.

"One of the women I worked with noticed the signs that I was battered. She convinced me to secretly go to another lady, a doctor who helps abused women. I couldn't go often, but after a few years I learned that I didn't have to live my life in constant terror." She ducked her head. "It took a bit longer for me to gather my courage and work out my escape."

Cadeyrn stroked her arm. "What he did, 'tis why you dinnae trust men."

"I've never really known any men except my father. He kept me locked up in his mansion most of the time. He hired tutors and governesses to look after me. God only knows what he did to my mother while I was kept away from her. He stopped her from seeing me altogether, which I think is when she gave up any hope she had left." She dragged in a stuttering breath. "One night she went to take a bath, and instead hung herself with the belt of her robe."

Cadeyrn pulled her close and held her until she felt steady enough to continue.

"I got away, and took a job as a sous-chef on a ship. I'd only been free of my father for six months when Coig took me from my time. I didn't try to fight him off. I watched him kill a man with one blow." Her voice shook so badly she gulped. "I could do nothing, but it wasn't because of my father. I was completely paralyzed. Coig squeezed too hard when he grabbed me, and—"

"He broke your neck." Cadeyrn touched her mouth with his fingertips. "I saw what he did to you in my dreams." He slid his hand around her neck to cup her nape. "Night after night I relived it, there but no' there. Helpless to stop that facking brute from hurting you."

Lily didn't know what to think, so she pushed on.

"When I came to your time, my neck wasn't broken anymore. I could move again. Coig saw that and tried to throttle me, but another guard stopped him. Since then he's been hurting me, much worse than my father ever did. It brought back so many horrid memories that I couldn't bear..." She stared at her hands. "I couldn't go through it again. Not after I worked so hard to escape one monster. So, I began plotting to get in the druids' good graces and make them believe I'd help them find your clan. At first it was to stop Coig from hurting me, but then I knew what I really wanted."

He made a low, soft sound. "Revenge."

"I wanted Coig to suffer, and I still want it," she admitted. "They don't bleed, him and his kind, but they can be hurt. I want him to feel all the misery that he's caused me, and more."

"'Twill no' take away your pain," Cadeyrn said and tucked her head under his chin. "As a man I went in search of the Pritani lad who falsely accused me and caused me so much injury. I found him in a grave. I felt so cheated. An older lady saw me as she came to lay flowers on the spot. She wept as she told me her son had been killed by brigands for his horse and his boots. She swore to me that he'd been a good lad, and provided for her and her family, even in the lean times."

"What did you tell her?"

"I said that I'd learned much from him." His mouth hitched. "'Twas the truth, of sorts. He taught me never to lie, or steal, or blame another for wrongs I'd inflicted."

"I wish I could be as brave as you are. When I came here, I wanted to die." She pressed her hand over his chest to feel the strong beating of his heart. "The others are the reason I didn't kill myself. I thought, if I could just do something, and get them back to our time, then maybe I could go on living. I could be free again. Only there's nothing waiting for me in the future but a broken neck."

"But you said the portal healed you," Cadeyrn said, his hand sliding over her nape.

"In this time, yes." She met his gaze. "Hendry told me that if we go back through the portal, it reverses any healing it gave us when we came here. The moment I step into my time, my neck will break, and I'll be completely paralyzed. Even if I manage to survive that, I'll be trapped in a useless body for the rest of my life."

"Then you never return," he said, his voice hard now. "You stay here, in my time, with me."

She ducked her head. "I don't want your pity, mate. What happened to me was wretched, but I don't belong here at all. Maybe returning is the proper punishment for what I've done to you."

"For convincing me to come here and help you rescue three ladies stolen by our enemy? No, lass," he chided. "'Twas a brave and daring thing you did. When we return to Dun Mor, my chieftain shall reward you."

"But don't you see it? I did exactly to you what the mad druids did to me. And I'm—I'm so sorry, truly I am." She buried her face in her palms.

"Have it as you will. Since you wish to be punished, as your victim I should choose how." He tugged her hands away from her face and brought her up against him. "You shall remain and serve me. You must kiss me often when we're alone, and call me your mate and your boyo, always. I'll want your hands on me as well. Very often. Your touch pleases me."

Could it be possible that he'd forgiven her? No, Lily never had that sort of luck. "You're laughing at me."

"Do I sound as if I jest?" he demanded sternly. "I've more than I wish as recompense. At night you must sleep naked beside me. No, I think atop me. I very much like that, and feeling your breath on my face while you are sleeping. Shagging before we sleep shall not be required, but greatly encouraged."

A laugh burst from her lips. "You want me to stay and be your pleasure lass? Are you mad?"

"I want you, Lily Stover." He tipped up her chin and brushed his mouth over her trembling lips. "By my side, in my bed, and with me, always, as my lady.

A bubble of joy began to grow inside her. "You'll have to lie to your clan—to your chieftain."

He lifted his shoulders. "I need no' tell them exactly how you convinced me to help you. Or when."

Lily recalled how serious Cadeyrn had been when he'd told her that he never lied. "If anyone finds out, they may never trust either of us again. Can you live with that, mate?"

Cadeyrn kissed her brow. "For you, aye."

Chapter Thirteen

I N THE COLD gray hours before dawn Brennus lay awake beside his sleeping wife. Since Cadeyrn had gone missing he'd tried to think like his war master. He'd spent long hours endeavoring to craft some clever plan. To bring home his brother and, if he'd found them, the lasses held by the *famhairean* would strike a great blow against the mad druids. Yet nothing had come to Brennus but more worry and frustration. He knew himself to be a man of actions, not schemes, but now he saw his own lacking only too plainly.

He'd chosen Cadeyrn as his second because he possessed what Brennus lacked: a gift for strategy.

Nor could he rely on the magic folk. Already he'd waited too long for word from the insufferable Bhaltair Flen. If Ruadri had not sent news by now, it would come too late, if it came at all.

No, Brennus thought. If it was aid he needed, it must come from himself.

Rising carefully so as not to disturb his lady, he pulled on his trews, boots, and tunic and left their chamber. Torches burned low in the wall brackets he passed, reminding him that with every day that passed the likelihood of recovering Cadeyrn dwindled. His footsteps echoed in the empty stone passage as he made his way to Dun Mor's lowest subterranean level. There he stood before the clan's *caibeal*, the chapel which he and his men had filled with large stones carved to honor the Skaravens' battle spirits.

"I need your guidance more than ever," Brennus said, and stepped inside.

Entering the *caibeal* since Althea had come to Dun Mor always reminded Brennus to leave outside his arrogance. More than once the battle spirits had sent him to walk a path he would not have chosen. That the raven, his battle spirit, had brought to him a beautiful lady from a distant future seemed as incredible as what they'd found together. Had he not paid heed, he might have instead sent Althea away, and lost the chance to know the love of his life.

A pulsing, warm glow spread from the raven skinwork on his chest. But he knew it wasn't because he'd entered the sacred chapel. Though he didn't turn, he grinned.

"Though you are silent as the wind," he said, "you cannae catch me unawares, Wife."

"Then it's a good thing that's not what I'm doing," she said, coming beside him. "Mostly I'm wondering about how I'm always waking up before dawn lately." She took his hand. "Alone, most of the time."

"I couldnae sleep," he said. "And I didnae wish to wake you."

"Next time, wake me," she said, standing close. "I'm worried about them too." She peered into the dark interior. "Are you thinking what I'm thinking?"

He nodded. "I'll wait no longer."

Brennus moved through the darkness by
memory to the very heart of the *caibeal*. There
stood the largest of the stones, a black crystal
morion carved with the clan's raven symbol.
He and Althea knelt before it, as he bowed his
head and pressed his hand over the skinwork
inked beneath his left shoulder.

"I beg your help," Brennus said. "The
famhairean took from us our war master,
Cadeyrn. We dinnae ken to where, but he may
be with four lasses in desperate need of sanctuary and protection. Cadeyrn cannae prevail
alone against our enemy. The Skaraven stand
ready to fight for him, and the innocents
stolen from their time. I beseech you, tell me
where we may find them."

The eye of the raven carved on the
morion glowed with a fierce blue light that
illuminated Brennus and his lady. Beneath his
tunic his skinwork began to move, biting into
his flesh like the peck of a pointed beak.
Althea squirmed beside him, reaching a hand
behind her. He moved to rub her back where
she couldn't reach, when the light from the
carving winked out.

Even through their tunics, Brennus could see their skinwork light up with a dark blue glow. As Althea turned to him, her face was bathed in the glow from his ink. All around them the air moved, thick with ghostly spirits. Ravens that seemed to be made of smoke swirled around them and between them, sweeping Althea's hair to and fro as the wind from their wings buffeted them. As one, they spiraled upward, whirling like a dark storm above the crystal statue. They boiled this way and that, bulging toward the top, until two pointed years appeared, two empty holes for eyes, and a downturned beak below them.

"The owl," Brennus muttered. "'Tis Cadeyrn's battle spirit."

It stretched out its undulating wings, each feather a moving raven. But just as the enormous, roiling creature seemed to take flight, it cleaved in two.

"Gods," Althea exclaimed, as she clutched his arm.

As though an unseen axe descended from above, the wraithlike owl divided into halves. Ears, eyes, and wings leaned away from the center, falling in slow motion, to disappear into a hazy mist.

The eye of the raven carved on the morion glowed with a fierce blue light and then slowly faded away.

"As the Gods will," Brennus said, reaching out to touch the face of the crystal.

He helped Althea to her feet and they silently retreated from the chamber.

"What was that?" Althea said when they reached the stone passage. She glanced back over her shoulder. "I hope it doesn't mean what I think it means."

Though Brennus grimaced, he shook his head. "As ever, 'tis a puzzle within a puzzle. 'Tis often hard to see their meaning."

Though Althea was troubled by the vision granted them by the battle spirit, Brennus found new hope. Cadeyrn still lived. He knew it deep in his bones. He was as sure of it as if his war master had appeared.

"A puzzle," Althea said. "It figures. It's the kind of thing Cade could figure out, but he's not here."

Brennus came to a stop and stared at his wife. He had been thinking about this all wrong. He didn't need to wait for Cadeyrn. Nor did he need to strategize like his war master. What he needed was to think like his enemy.

"What?" Althea said. "Do I have ravens on my–"

"Come, Wife," he said grasping her hand and striding back to their chamber. He snatched down a parchment map from one of the shelves and spread it on the table.

"What are you looking for?" she asked, as she came to his side and gazed down at the map.

"'Tis not what I look for," he said, scanning back and forth. "'Tis what I dinnae look for."

"Okay," she said, hands on hips. "You've lost me."

"Hendry kens we travel by water. He expected us at the farm."

"Right, that's how we were ambushed."

"He'll no' make that mistake again," Brennus said.

Althea slowly nodded. "You're looking for an area without water."

His finger traced the tall ridges that

flanked deep valleys as they ran to the coast. "And where they believe themselves hidden."

In his mind's eye he could picture much of the terrain, but it was an image from twelve centuries past. Brennus had seen from their first approach to Dun Mor that, though the largest features of the land had not changed, much else had altered. Forests had come and gone, waterways had opened and closed, and some had even changed course. He leaned over the map, hands fisted on the table.

"I used to ken these lands like my own keep," he said, the old frustration over Bhaltair and his schemes returning.

"I wish we knew more about Scotland in this time," Althea muttered.

Brennus thought of a small but lethal mortal laird who had once proposed making Althea his bedding wench. He grinned at her. "I ken someone who does."

An hour later sentries escorted Brennus and Althea into Maddock McAra's castle. Althea took her husband's arm and leaned close.

"Don't mention Emeline," she said lowly. "They're almost spitting images of each other." When Brennus turned a puzzled look to her, she added, "I think they're related."

In the Great Hall, Maddock and his large family had gathered for their morning meal. The diminutive laird shot up from his chair as soon as he saw Brennus, and grinned as he came over to greet them.

"You seem determined to catch me at my leisure, Chieftain," the McAra laird scolded him. "Lady Althea, you look as fetching as a spring day. Come, break your fast with us."

Brennus felt a surge of impatience over the clan's social niceties, but he also valued Maddock as his strongest ally. With a glance at his lady, who nodded in silent agreement, they joined the family and dined with them on pottage, freshly-baked oat cakes and pear butter.

The laird spoke only of family matters at his table, inquiring of his wife as to her plans for the day, and his children as to their studies. Brennus felt slightly envious of Maddock whenever he came to the McAra stronghold, for the laird seemed so easy in his affections. Only when the family departed the hall did

Maddock's happy disposition sober to a shrewder graveness.

"My thanks for your patience," the laird said. "I ken you didnae visit to hear of my wife's plans for the solar. How may the McAra serve the Skaraven?"

"We believe the *famhairean* now hold our war master, Cadeyrn," Brennus said, and explained the circumstances. "We search for a place with no approach from water, and where the druids believe they and the giants can hide."

Maddock rubbed his mouth with the side of his finger. "No water, you say?" When Brennus nodded the laird called for his steward, and had the man bring a map of the McAra holdings.

Rolling out the scroll on the table, Maddock studied it before encircling a large area with his fingertip. "Here, where the land naturally rises and 'tis thick with forest." He pointed to a patch of criss-crossed plots. "The closest water lies in the farmland to the west. A small river feeds the mill where the farmers take their grain."

"Will you grant me leave to search those lands?" Brennus asked.

"Aye, if you'll permit the McAra to accompany you," the laird said, and grinned. "We maynae be immortal, but we're braw in a fight."

Chapter Fourteen

A S THE SUN began to set Cadeyrn climbed to the back side of the crevasse to inspect the surrounding countryside. Another set of steps hewn into the rock face led out of the fortlet and down to the landscape below. He saw gleaned fields and empty roads leading into the hills, but no body of water he could use to take the ladies back to Dun Mor. There would be no easy escape. Though he harbored a hope that the druids and the giants had perished in the fire, he knew better than to rely on a hope. More than likely they were already looking for them. As war master, he had to assume it.

When he returned he found all of the women awake but Lily.

"Here, to warm you," Emeline said and brought him a clay cup filled with a steaming herb brew. "You must be exhausted."

"I've been trained to go a week without sleep, my lady," he told her, and sipped the hot drink, which had a distinct tang to it. "'Tis very good. Where did you find the sorrel?"

"Lily spotted a patch near the steps." The nurse glanced at his lady. "Can we give her another hour or two? She's barely slept in weeks."

He nodded as he gazed at Lily. "They'll no' send the guards out at night to search for us."

"Good," the healer replied looking relieved.

Though he knew it likely that the women would've seen little of the surrounding country, he needed every scrap of information that could be had.

"Do you ken of any lochs or rivers near the hills here?" he asked.

"Not close," Rowan said as she came over to join them. "I heard Hendry tell his nutjob wife that he got fresh horses from a village on the other side of the hills. He said he'd put something in the pond there, too, but I couldn't make out what it was. Probably poison, knowing him. Why do you need a body of water?"

"For traveling to my clan's stronghold," Cadeyrn said and dipped his fingers in the cup. He showed the ladies how they turned transparent. "Once I bond with a river or loch, I can move through it, and take you with me."

"You're selkies?" Emeline exclaimed, gaping at him.

"Something like them," he said, "only we dinnae turn into seals."

"Would a big puddle work?" Rowan said. "I'll melt the snow." She grimaced as he shook his head. "Crap. That would have been really convenient."

"We'll cross the hills tonight," Cadeyrn told her, "and use the village pond."

"Lily needs more sleep first," Emeline said firmly. "I expect even with all your training, you could benefit from a short nap, too."

"I'll keep watch while you're down," Rowan said, wrapping herself in a piece of his tartan.

Cadeyrn considered refusing, but the warrior in him knew to eat and sleep when he could. There was no knowing when he'd have the chance again. But it was the wave of comforting warmth from Emeline that pushed him toward Lily.

"Wake us before moonrise," he said, before he stretched out beside Lily, pulled her close, and closed his eyes.

At some point during their nap Lily rolled over to nestle against him. Half-awake, he curled an arm around her waist and stroked her back. A short time later her eyelashes fluttered, and she tilted her head back.

"You're in bed with me again."

"I cannae keep from you," he murmured and pressed his mouth to her brow. "And 'twas cold."

"So I'm to be your personal warming blanket now too." Her lips curved into a rare smile. "I wish we were alone, boyo."

Emeline cleared her throat. "So do I," she muttered as she came to stand over them. "I'll fetch Rowan, then."

When they all gathered, Cadeyrn surveyed them. "We must cross the hills, and 'twill be dangerous. Lily and I shall walk lead. Emeline, you follow behind us. Rowan, you and Perrin shall have our backs. Watch your footfalls and keep silent. Emeline, if 'tis need to stop and rest, touch my forearm."

He made sure to wrap them as best he could in the pieces of his tartan before guiding them out of the back side of the fortlet. The brisk night wind whirled away the white clouds of their breaths, and the snow and ice promised to make their trek a miserable one.

"Walking will keep us warm," Lily told him as they made their way down the steps. "And we really are stronger than you think."

The drifts outside the crevasse proved mercifully shallow, and after the first mile they left behind the snow altogether. Some of the ancient trails left by the Ninth Legion remained intact, although strewn and rocky, and then they met the next slopes and began their climb.

Cadeyrn kept glancing back at Emeline until the nurse scowled at him. She might be hurt and weary and breathing too fast, but she seemed determined to keep up with him.

After they scaled the second hill Cadeyrn

felt a surge of relief, for the path down led to a narrow glen and into a small village. He saw the moonlight gleaming on the still surface of a pond behind a large shearing barn, and knew Dun Aran to finally be within their reach.

He signaled for the other women to halt as he scanned the trees on either side of the road. Remembering all too well how the *famhairean* had tricked them on the path to the forest farm, he motioned for Lily and the others to stay while he crept ahead. Happily, none of the trees lining the road turned into the giants, and he doubled back at a fast trot.

"'Tis safe," he murmured, and saw the same relief he felt on their faces. "Everyone in the village will be abed. We'll go directly to the pond."

Cadeyrn dared to take Lily's hand in his as they walked the final distance to reach the village. No lights illuminated the cottages, and when they reached the shearing barn he saw only an empty pen that had been left open. But then the faintest stink of rot reached his nose. 'Twas a stench he knew only too well.

He motioned for the women to stop next to the barn.

"Remain here for a moment," Cadeyrn told them, and released Lily's hand to walk down to the pond.

The surface glittered with what he thought at first was frost, and then he saw the things sticking up out of the dark ice. The pond had been too shallow to cover all the bodies of the murdered villagers, so hands and limbs and heads protruded. When he knelt to touch the frozen water, he sensed only ice stretching to the very bottom.

"Hey, what's the hold up?" Rowan asked from behind him, and when he turned he saw her face blanch in the moonlight. "Oh, no, no."

"Dinnae look at it," he said as he took her arm. He turned her around and guided her back up to the barn. To the other lasses he said, "We cannae go into the pond. 'Tis frozen solid, and…'tis been used as a grave for the villagers."

Emeline stared at him before she staggered backward, spun around and ran behind a bush, from where the sound of retching came.

"Hendry killed all the people who lived here?" Perrin asked. "The women and the children, too?" When he nodded she turned to her sister. "This has to stop. Someone has to stop them."

"Yeah, I know, but not tonight." Rowan glanced to the east before she regarded Cadeyrn. "The sun's going to rise soon. What'll we do now?"

He knew the ladies all to be exhausted. He could see it in the way they stood hunched and breathed hard. They'd had almost nothing to eat, and but a few hours of sleep. He knew they'd keep going for as long as he asked. In truth, they'd go until they dropped, which would not take long to happen.

"We'll stay here and hide for the day." He looked around the village until he spotted the largest of the cottages. Shutters covered the window openings to keep out the snow, and would help conceal their presence. "There."

Emeline came out from behind the bush and limped to a stop. "I agree. Mostly because Lily can't feel her feet anymore, and I think I just sprained my ankle."

"Can you walk?" Cadeyrn asked, seeing

how she put most of her weight on the other foot.

She nodded quickly. "I'll run if I have to."

The war master turned to his lady. "Why didnae you tell me about your feet?"

"I was planning to warm them at your Dun Mor." She sighed. "Tell me we can light a fire, and I'll toast them while I make us some food."

In the wind that had driven the snow storm, a small fire could be permitted. Though he suspected the other women were just as tired and half-frozen as Lily and Emeline, for their safety it could not be.

"I'm sorry, no," he said, and saw each of their faces fall. "But we'll find blankets and a meal before we sleep."

As they waited in the growing light, he went into the big cottage to assure it was empty. Then he left the women there to search the rest of the village. He entered a large stable he expected to be empty, but instead found eleven work horses that the druids had left to starve in their stalls. Cadeyrn filled their troughs with just enough water to quench their thirst, and then portioned out the feed he found sacked in a wall bin. As the hungry horses ate he inspected each one. More than half proved too old to serve as mounts, but enough were healthy and strong enough for him and his ladies to ride.

As he left the stable, Cadeyrn glanced up at the fading stars. Ruadri would urge him to give thanks for the horses he'd found, but surely it had been by chance, not the Gods' will.

In the villagers' homes he found signs of countless, desperate struggles. Directly outside of them dried blood still marked the earth with red-brown splatters and frozen pools. From what he saw it seemed the *famhairean* had dragged out every mortal from their beds and killed them outside before tossing their bodies in the pond. The merciless indifference the giants showed toward mortal life stoked in him a furious sorrow. Before this moment he had always regarded the druids and their *famhairean* as the clan's enemies. Now he understood what they would make of the world—blood and bodies and death—and it chilled him.

As war master, so much of Cadeyrn's own life had been spent in anger and suspicion.

He'd been bred to brutality and the company of other warriors. If he'd gone down a different path, could this empty village have been his work?

Walking to the center of the small settlement, he went down on one knee. While he gave the Gods their due, his true devotion belonged to his battle spirit. He covered his skinwork with one hand.

"Too long I've been blinded by the wrongs of the past. Help me see clearly, that I protect and serve, not only my lady, but humankind."

Strength poured into his veins, answering him as directly as he could have hoped. Cadeyrn murmured his thanks as he pressed his palms to the ground. Then he stood and went back to the big cottage. Inside he found the ladies gathered around a small table set with food.

"I found horses. Tonight, we ride."

"First, we eat, and then we sleep," Rowan said. "And then we'll ride with you into the sunset." When Emeline frowned at her she shrugged. "Okay, so it's a terrible cliché in our time. In this one, it actually fits."

The healer glanced in the direction of the

pond, and then at Cadeyrn. "Not much more we can do, I imagine."

He grimaced and silently shook his head.

Perrin offered him a plate of bread chunks. "Lily's in the kitchen putting together a cold platter."

Cadeyrn smiled his thanks as he took a piece of the crusty bread, and then touched Emeline's shoulder.

"When the thaw comes, my clan shall return and see to them."

Though she still looked pained, Emeline nodded.

He took a bite of the bread on his way to the kitchen, and found it had been cut in half, the middle filled with thick slabs of butter and slathered with a berry jam. He discovered his lady cutting up roots and vegetables, which she then added to a pan of meat sliced so thin he could almost see through it. He'd never seen Lily move with such ease of purpose, but he also suspected that what she did kept her from thinking about the bodies in the pond.

The lasses each had their ways of coping with the worst of times: Emeline nursed,

Rowan jested, Perrin ate, and Lily fed them all.

He glanced down at her feet, and smiled a little at the heavy, too-large boots she now wore.

"What happened to your shoes?"

"They're in the trash bin. I'm never taking off these clodhoppers for as long as I draw breath." Regret flickered over her features. "I shouldn't have said that. Not at all respectful."

"'Tis no' wrong to be happy that you live," he chided.

"But it's not about me, is it?" She halved a small bitter orange and squeezed the juice into the pan. "We can't do anything for those poor people. I thought about using my trick to crack the ice and get them out, but the ground's too frozen to dig graves. We're eating their food and stealing their shoes and clothes, and we can't even give them a decent burial."

"They wouldnae begrudge us any of it, Lily," he said.

"I know." Her hands stopped moving for a moment as she glanced up at him. "It's just another thing to hate. I'm so bloody tired of hating, Cade."

"Then you must look past it." He grazed her cheek with his knuckles. "See what awaits you."

Her expression softened. "Three starved women."

Smiling, she picked up the pan and handed it to him. She took a platter spread with sliced cheeses, candied fruits, and small bowls of nuts. Together they carried them into the front room.

"I haven't a stove," she said to the other women as she checked the pan before bringing it to the table. "But this should be better than chestnuts."

"Carpaccio?" Rowan said, her jaw nearly dropping.

The women eagerly fell to serving themselves, as did Cadeyrn. Though he didn't know the strange food, the flavors came alive in his mouth as he chewed. He'd never tasted the like, and it proved so delectable that it made him wonder what other talents his lady possessed.

"How did you make this?"

Lily met his gaze. "The acid from the

citrus cooks the raw meat. If we had lemons it would be better."

"Oh, no, this is perfect," Perrin assured her as she stuffed a huge piece of the cured and thin-sliced beef into her mouth. "This is amazing. I love you. Marry me."

"You'll have to fight me," Cadeyrn said, making everyone laugh.

"Lovely to know I'm so wanted," Lily told them.

Cadeyrn waited until all the ladies had taken another portion before he loaded up a plate. "I'll have this outside while I'm on watch."

Lily nodded, some of the lightness leaving her expression, and the rest of the ladies fell silent.

Outside Cadeyrn found a sheltered spot that gave him the best view of the road leading in and out of the village, and there slowly savored Lily's carpaccio. Like pleasure, food for him had always been a necessity, not a desire. She had changed that now, too, and he would likely never taste another trencher of beef without thinking of this night, and watching her cook.

A shadow crossed his as Lily came to him. "You didn't wait for the drinks, mate." She offered the bottle in her hand to him.

He uncorked it, took a sniff and handed it back. "Dinnae tell my clan, but I've never much cared for whiskey."

"You might have to resign your citizenship for that," she chided, her gaze straying from him to the shearing barn. "The people here were sleeping when Hendry came with the guards, weren't they?" When he nodded, her mouth flattened. "He could have just stolen the horses. Why did he have them all killed?"

He put his arm around her hunched shoulders. "Hendry and Murdina have long despised mortal and druid kind. They hold them to blame for the loss of their tribe. 'Twas said that they and the *famhairean* murdered more than could be counted in my time."

"Your time?" She looked up at him. "You mean you don't belong here? Were you brought here, like us?"

Cadeyrn nodded. "I lived and died twelve centuries past. Like you, the druids brought me here without my say. Those who awakened me and my clan from our graves intended for us to again battle the *famhairean*. They gave us immortality, and our ability to water-travel, but naught of it we wished or wanted."

"Good God." She uncorked the bottle and took a long drink from it, coughing a little once she'd swallowed. "I see now why you don't like whiskey. It's absolutely vile."

"I favor perry." He rubbed her back as she coughed again. "'Tis made from pear juice."

"I make a wonderful tart with pears poached in brandy. You'd love every bite." She curled her hand around his and looked out at the village. "Only we're not going to get away, Cade. I don't think we can make it."

"We've horses now, so we've a chance." He wouldn't tell her how tiny it was. "With food and rest the lasses should have more strength tonight. We'll press on north until we find water."

She set the bottle on the window ledge. "Who knows how far we'll have to go to find water than isn't frozen, maybe miles and miles. I had some riding lessons when I was younger, but I doubt the others have. Emeline and Perrin won't admit it, but they're completely exhausted. I'm hardly in tip-top shape, either.

You and Rowan can't manage the three of us between you. If we have to keep riding for the whole night…"

"'Twas much the same for you with your father, I reckon, and yet you escaped him." Cadeyrn took her in his arms. "Hardship and evil can take all from you. But your belief in yourself? That you must give."

"Well, then." She stood on her toes to kiss his mouth, and then held him tightly. "Sod that."

Chapter Fifteen

＊＊＊

L EAVING ORIANA AND the Dawn Fire at the Moss Dapple's settlement worried Bhaltair almost as much as Galan's admitted cruelty toward his son. He'd accepted sanctuary for his tribe from druids far too suspicious and secretive for his taste. The headman's venomous hatred for Ruadri, who had made only the mistake of being born, also preyed on his conscience. Not once during the training of the Skaraven lads had Galan's son ever revealed the maltreatment from his sire. It made him wonder what else had been hidden from him. Though he grimaced at the deeply troubling thought, at present there was naught that he could do.

Dealing with the quislings and their *famhairean* had to come before all other concerns.

As Domnall stood by, Bhaltair quickly read the small batch of message scrolls.

"No sign of the Skaraven or the enemy," Bhaltair said. He glanced up at the overseer's impassive expression. "As well you ken."

"The headman wishes all things that enter and leave the forest checked," Domnall told him. "I've no belly for trickery, Master. I but do as Galan commands."

"You sound like a mortal," Bhaltair said. He suspected the overseer wished to say more but would not permit himself to confide in an outsider. He also seemed to cling to his stoic indifference like a shield. But against what? "Are you compelled by Galan to act against your own reason, Domnall?"

He considered that for a long moment. "'Tis my duty to serve the headman. I give my loyalty freely."

So, it would seem that Galan had not used magic to force the overseer and his defenders to obey him.

"But he trained you."

"To protect this settlement." Domnall's

mouth hitched. "Aye."

Bhaltair decided against asking any more questions. The overseer might report his interest to Galan, who might then act against the Dawn Fire. Instead he only nodded.

"I must leave now to journey to Aviemore. Overseer, I'd consider it a boon if you'd watch over my people and attend to their needs until I return."

Domnall bowed. "As you wish, Master."

The overseer escorted him to the falls, where he stopped at the passage into the cascade and untethered the chestnut steed that waited there.

"Safe journey, Bhaltair Flen."

"My thanks, Domnall." He pulled up his hood, took the reins, and stepped into the tunnel.

Some hours later Bhaltair arrived in Aviemore, which remained dark and quiet in the hour before dawn. He climbed down wearily from his mount and held onto the saddle horns until his knees steadied. The sleepy stablemaster appeared and muttered under his breath as he took the pony's tether.

"Water and brush him, and change his

blanket," Bhaltair told the mortal, and handed him enough coin to silence his grumbling. "I'll return for him in a few hours."

Since he yet saw no sign of Ruadri he went to the inn where they had agreed to meet and made his way to the kitchen.

The innkeeper's wife looked up from the pot of oatmeal she stirred, her surprise plain. "Fair morning, Master Flen. You've put my rooster to shame. Will you be wanting a room?"

"No' this day, Mistress Moray." He forced a smile. "I'm to meet a friend here for a short talk. We'll use your back room, if we may."

"'Tis your friend a grand brawny high-lander?" She held a hand high above her head, and then measured a broad space in the air equally impressive. "Silvered black hair and eyes like smoke?" When he nodded she let out a breath. "He came an hour back, drip-ping wet. Said he slipped and fell in the loch."

"The lad can be clumsy," Bhaltair said, nodding.

"I put him to wait in the back room and lit the fire." Her mouth twisted. "Such an odd man. He barely spoke to me."

She was likely but the second female Ruadri had ever spoken to. "You ken how highlanders can be." He peeked at her pot. "If you can spare two bowls of your lovely porridge to break our fast, I'll be in your debt."

"After all the coin you've dropped in my purse?" She waved a hand at him. "I'll bring it along with some berries and cream, just as you like it."

Bhaltair smiled his thanks and trudged down a passage to the back room, where he found Ruadri crouched by the hearth.

The big man straightened and faced him. "Cadeyrn?"

"We've yet had no word of him or the lost ladies. I sent word from the Moss Dapple's settlement by dove to all the tribes." He sat down with a grunt. "We cannae yet give up hope."

The shaman peered down at him. "Then I shall tell you my news, Master Flen. The clan found the hidden portal in the Great Wood."

"What? How?" he demanded.

"The lass who came to take Cadeyrn used it." Ruadri went to brace an arm on the mantle and stare into the flames. "I've said naught to Brennus about it, or how I've used it to come to you with my reports."

A knock sounded on the door, and Mistress Moray came in with bowls of her porridge and two mugs of morning brew. Smiling at Ruadri, she set the meal down on the table before bobbing a curtsey and departing.

"Come and sit," Bhaltair invited. "You can tell me everything while we eat."

"I've but to tell you this." The big man turned to face him. "I can use the portal to search for Cadeyrn."

Bhaltair knew what the lad was about to propose. "I cannae permit it. 'Twould expose your druid training to the clan."

"I ken that." Ruadri closed his eyes. "I'll go alone to find him, and send word back through the portal before I confront the *famhairean*."

"But alone against them, that 'twould be… no," he said flatly. "I'll no' send you to your death. Lad, how can you think of wasting the great gift we've bestowed on you?"

"*Gift*, you call it." The shaman turned and

strode over to snatch him out of his chair. "I'm a traitor to my clan. I've been thus my entire life. So much betrayal clings to me I wear shame like my skin."

Was that how Ruadri thought of his sacred duty? What had Galan put in his head?

"'Tis no' so. As you are, you still serve your clan. You watch over them, for their good as well as the good of mortal and druid kind."

"I ken exactly what I am," the shaman told him. "I spent my boyhood being beaten and ill-used and reviled by my own sire. He fashioned me into your creature. I've swallowed my disgust all this time to keep my clan safe, but it doesnae change what I am." He lowered Bhaltair back to the chair and knelt before him. "After I'm gone the clan shall never ken what I was. Permit me end my slavery by saving my brother. I beg you."

He'd never seen such torment as he beheld in Ruadri's eyes. "I shall release you from your duties as Watcher." He held up one hand. "If you shall vow to me in return that you willnae go near that portal, or by other means attempt to end your life."

The shaman's broad shoulders sagged. "I

never thought you as cruel as my sire. 'Twas another mistake of mine."

As Ruadri covered his eyes with one huge hand Bhaltair touched his arm. "What your father…what Galan did to you, 'twas born of grief. Losing your mother twisted his mind and darkened his heart. Only ken that the harm he inflicted on you, he did in secret. 'Tis why he insisted he alone train you, I reckon, so I and the other druids should no' learn of it—and we never did."

The shaman let his hand drop to stare at him. "Then how could you ken of it?"

Bhaltair silently cursed himself for stepping into a trap of his own making. "Galan spoke of it to me after I told him we had awakened your clan. He shall be made to answer for it, Ruadri."

"But no' while your tribe takes sanctuary with his," the shaman said bitterly, and then turned his head and rose to his feet. He moved silently to the door, opening it quickly, and a small cloaked figure stumbled inside. "The next time you sneak about, dinnae lean against the door. That makes it creak."

"I wasnae sneaking," Oriana said as she

tugged back her hood. "I but wished to ken if my master had finished with you."

Bhaltair rubbed his brow. "Lass, what do you here?"

"Forgive me, Master, but I couldnae remain behind when you might need me. 'Tis much I may do to serve you and our cause." She regarded the shaman with a far less contrite expression. "Unlike some I might name."

Ruadri looked perplexed, while Bhaltair said quickly, "I'm touched by your willingness, my dear one, but 'tis far too dangerous now to accompany me. You must go back to the forest."

The young druidess's lower lip trembled. "But you vowed that I would be your acolyte. I cannae learn from you if I'm no' at your side."

"'Tis no' a time for teaching, Mistress Embry," Ruadri told her, sounding tired. "Return to my sire's settlement. He and his tribe shall keep you safe."

"You think I care naught for any but myself, as you do?" Oriana spat her words at him. "The *famhairean* tortured and murdered my beloved Gwyn. He died because you and your clan of craven bastarts turned your backs on us. My master brought you back to the world for one purpose: to battle our enemy." She shrieked the words now, her hands balled into tight little fists. "He gave you the greatest gift any mortal could dream of so to aid you, and you ran away like cowards."

The silence that stretched out seemed to throb like Bhaltair's knee. He closed his eyes briefly before he said to Ruadri, "I'll have your word, lad, and give you mine."

The shaman nodded, and after a final long look at Oriana, left them alone.

"Come here to me, my dear one." When Oriana trudged over to him Bhaltair took hold of her hands. "Attend me now. Your grandfather has gone, but he shall return, as will we all. Only our bodies die. Gwyn isnae lost to you. Someday a young lad will walk up to you and greet you as his granddaughter."

All the rigid tension seemed to drain out of her. "I cannae bear this world without him, Master."

"For now, you must," he said firmly. "Shouting at Ruadri willnae change what happened to your grandfather. You've every right to be hurt, but you cannae lay the blame for it on the clan. 'Tis dangerous to call the Skaraven cowards and bastarts. They're a proud clan, and have every reason to be so. If word of what you said reached their chieftain's ears... Brennus would take great offense. Such a thing could cause a rift between us that I might never repair."

"So, we must coddle them," she said dully.

"I cherish them as our only hope," Bhaltair reproved gently. "For all our magics and wisdom, we cannae prevail over the giants. Naught but the Skaraven can." He took one bowl and placed it in her hands. "We shall break our fast together, and then I shall ride with you to the portal."

"Please dinnae send me back to the Moss Dapple." Before he could reply Oriana added, "Yesterday their headman took me aside and asked me if I could channel the mortal dead. When I told him no, he grew angry. I tried to stay away from him, but...I think he might hurt me if I dinnae give him what he desires, Master."

Bhaltair realized this to be the true reason

she'd left the settlement. Speak-seers never tried to commune with the spirits of the mortal dead, as they were always crazed and violent when dragged back from the place of their afterlife. Galan knew that, but in his grief had attempted to impose his desires on Oriana anyway. The result would do even more harm to the lass.

"'Twas good that you came to me, then." He patted her hand. "We shall take rooms at the inn here until I make other provisions for you."

"To be at your side restores me like naught else," Oriana said quietly. "For you are my cherished hope, Master Flen. The greatest boon of my life has been the wisdom and guidance you've given me."

Bhaltair made a dismissive gesture but couldn't help but be pleased by her fervent admissions. He had sorely missed Cailean Lusk since his departure, but this wee lass might yet prove to be the ovate's equal.

"Doubtless it shall help me to sleep through a night entire," he told her. "Now, eat your porridge before it grows cold."

Chapter Sixteen

LILY FOUND A blanket for Emeline, who had claimed the narrow pallet in the back of the kitchen. "You should take my bed. I'd be jolly good here."

"I tried it, and it's too soft. When I get home, I'll have to find a barn to sleep in." The nurse sighed as she huddled beneath the warm wool, her long black braid hanging over the pallet's side almost to the floor. "I wish you could come back with us."

A week ago, she would have agreed. "Sleep well, Emeline."

From the kitchen Lily padded silently to the bed chamber near the front room, which had an open doorway. Through it she glanced in on Perrin, who had already fallen asleep beside her sister. Rowan opened her eyes for a moment before she gave Lily a thumbs-up.

Still on guard duty, Lily thought, and returned the gesture. *She puts the sentries at Buckingham to shame.*

Rowan's devotion to her sister made Lily feel envious. No one had ever loved her like that, except perhaps her mother, but she'd been too afraid of Edgar to fight for her. Another thing her father had stolen from her.

An empty bed awaited her in the room adjoining the sisters', but Lily still felt too restless to have a kip. She walked to stand before the largest door at the end of the hall. They'd all insisted Cadeyrn get some sleep as soon as the sun rose, and he'd finally agreed when they'd threatened to stay awake until he did.

Listening for any sound that would tell her Cadeyrn was still up, Lily felt rather foolish. She should leave him to it and try to settle down herself. Tonight, they'd set out on another long, grueling jaunt, and he'd need her to help him with the other women. They'd have to be on the lookout for the guards and the mad druids while they searched for the water that he'd promised would get them out. After everything she'd seen since coming to this time, Lily didn't doubt it, but what would come after they reached safety still troubled her.

Sleep wasn't what she needed.

Slipping inside, Lily stood for a moment to let her eyes adjust to the darkness. The couple who had lived in the big cottage had elected not to put windows in their bed chamber, which had been furnished with a large bed and little more. Cadeyrn lay on his side on the bed and, judging by his bare chest and arms, he'd stripped to his skin. She couldn't quite make out his clever features, but she already knew how they looked when he slept. With his guard down and the hard lines smoothed away, he had the face of a prince. Though she ached to go to him, he was sleeping.

As I should be.

But when Lily started to turn away, the scars on her arms tingled. She glanced back at Cadeyrn and saw the ink on his arm taking on a soft blue glow. The compulsion to be with him only grew stronger, almost tugging her to the side of the bed. The closer she drew, the warmer she felt.

With him is the only place I belong now.

His golden eyes opened, but before he could speak she pressed her fingertips against his mouth. She couldn't put what was happening into words, at least not that would make any sense, and he might send her away. Lily stepped back and took off her clothes.

Watching her, Cadeyrn propped himself on his elbow, and pulled back the linens. Once she'd climbed into bed he gathered her against him, and the feel of his body against hers made her think of a razor-edged knife sheathed in silk velvet. The moment she touched him some of his ink's glow seeped into her hand and raced up to pulse in her scars with cool blue light.

Finally, finally.

Lily put her hand to his face, tracing the angles and curves under his skin. Her fingertips found no flaws, and when she swept her thumb over his dark brow he dragged the edge of his teeth over the heel of her hand. He kissed her wrist before grasping it, and glided his mouth along her forearm to the inner bend of her elbow. That brought her breasts against the hard muscles of his chest, and her nipples pebbled so tightly in response she gasped.

Cadeyrn looked at her naked breasts for a long moment before he rolled onto his back and lifted her over him. His strong arms shifted her up until one peak grazed his mouth, and he enveloped it.

Watching him feast on her breast aroused her almost as much as feeling the wet, hot tug of his mouth. Lily brought her knees up to his sides and worked her hand under his head, pressing him against her throbbing mound as he licked and sucked.

Between her thighs his shaft hardened and swelled, and she shamelessly rocked against him, stroking both of them as desire bloomed thick and wet between her thighs. His mouth travelled from one breast to the other, which he lavished with the same hungry attention before he released her peak and looked up at her.

In that moment Lily fell into his gaze. The room around them faded as the blue glow from their arms took on a blinding brightness. It brought them together in a way she'd never before felt, as if his battle spirit stripped away all the outer trappings of what they were. Her eyes filled with what wasn't and yet what had always been, in the secret part of him that no one but she could see.

She gasped at what was there.

A huge castle made of immense golden stones towered in the midst of an endless desert. The air around the structure shimmered like a mirage and smelled of his heat. Shadows and light passed over the outer walls, revealing countless carvings of his eyes in the stones. The fortress stared back at her, enormous and unmovable, with only one gate built of bronze bars as thick as her body. At the base of the walls hundreds of owl-headed sentries stood, each armed with a sword and a club with a raven carved around the huge end.

Part of her understood the inexplicable sight. This was what lay inside him, this remote, guarded palace where he had always dwelled alone.

This is his fortress, but where is Cade?

Lily glanced down to see her body glowing in the hard sunlight. Although she'd never pranced about starkers, being naked here felt right. She ignored the menacing sentries and walked up to the massive gates. Looking in a narrow gap between the bars, she saw Cadeyrn standing inside, a huge sword held ready in his hands. He wore nothing but a cloak of white feathers that hung from his shoulders. Dark streaks painted on the cloak formed four words.

Bren, Ru, Ka, Tran. Across his bare chest she saw another word scrawled in dark gold: *Lily.*

Could this be some imagining of his heart? If it was, she suspected that she couldn't say anything to him that would convince him to let her inside. He'd guarded this place for so long that no one and nothing could ever breech its defenses. Then she felt something on her arms, and looked down to see sprouting from her flesh the same white feathers that made Cadeyrn's cloak. When they grew to a pair of wide, powerful wings, Lily knew what she had to do.

I'm coming, love.

She moved away from the gate, turning her back on her lover's fortress as she walked out into the darkness.

Dinnae go, lass.

Was that what he thought she was doing? Lily turned and began to run to him, lifting her arms as she did so that the icy air streamed under them. Just before she reached the gates she jumped as high as she could, and felt her body go weightless as she soared up and over the outer wall. She laughed as she flew up, riding the air currents as if she'd done nothing else her entire existence. When she glanced down she saw Cadeyrn staring up at her, his eyes wide.

Drawing in her wings, Lily flipped and began spiraling down until she encircled him. He snatched her out of the air, holding her tightly as she enveloped him with her feathery arms. All around them the walls began to fall, dissolving into piles of dust, and the sentries gathered around them, their weapons tumbling to the ground.

Cadeyrn drew his hands down the length of her wings, and the feathers vanished, leaving her flesh bare and warmed by his touch. She reached for his cloak, pushing it off his shoulders before she twined her arms around his neck.

You don't have to be here anymore, Lily thought,

pressing close to him. *Wherever you are, I'll always come to you. I'll storm your castles and kick down your walls and even fight my way through your owl-men if I must.*

He understood her perfectly, for he drew her hand down to his heart.

Then I'm yours, my lady.

The sky above them turned to starry black silk, and the sentries bowed as the darkness descended. Lily held onto Cadeyrn as the blue light showered over them, and then they lay facing each other in the bed back at the cottage. Their bodies remained naked, and as the glow faded tears spilled from her eyes. Everything she'd seen and experienced inside him had been real. She'd flown to him, and freed him from his lonely heart—as he'd done for her.

Whatever happened, from this moment on, they would always have each other.

Cadeyrn's hands cradled her face as he kissed away each tear, his mouth tender. The touch of his lips made her body heat, and urgency spike. She turned, tugging him atop her and clasping him between her legs. She didn't want to wait, she couldn't wait another second, and then he put his hand under her bottom and lifted her to him. He came into her with one slow, aching stroke, his heavy cock filling the last of her emptiness. When he'd buried himself in her, Cadeyrn touched his brow to hers.

They didn't need words anymore, Lily thought, feeling the ferocious need coiling in his muscles. He wanted to ravish her, hard and deep and without mercy, and it made her clench around him as her softness went liquid. When his golden eyes burned into hers, she nodded.

He uttered a low, tearing sound as he drew out of her, and then plowed back into her pussy. She felt the ridge of his cockhead dragging against her gripping hold a moment before she muffled a cry against his shoulder, and then they both lost control.

Lily's universe contracted to the two of them, their bodies caressing and colliding as they came together again and again. He fucked her so thoroughly she felt as if he'd become part of her body, his pumping shaft pummeling and pleasuring her until she shook uncontrollably. He caught her next cry with his mouth, swallowing it as he took her with his tongue and teeth and ravenous hunger. The bed bounced beneath her back, and then he came out of her and dragged her to the edge of it, flipping her over onto her belly and jerking up her hips as he planted his feet and surged into her again.

Yes, yes. She gripped the linens with tight fists. *Mate with me.*

Groaning into the ticking, Lily pushed back against his heavy thrusts, impaling herself on him as he reached for her breasts, and cupped them to squeeze her peaks. She felt her bottom bouncing and her thighs growing slick with their mingled fluids, but Cadeyrn didn't stop. He fucked Lily as if she was his universe, as if no other woman but her could please him, and realizing that pushed her over the edge.

A big hand covered her mouth as he pulled her back against him, going deep and holding her on his cock as she exploded. He grunted as she sank her teeth into his palm, and when she shuddered her last he jerked from her and rolled her onto her back, bringing her hand to his wet shaft and curling her fingers around it.

His eyes watched her pump him in her fist, his jaw so tight she thought it might crack. He straddled her, bringing his gleaming cockhead close to her breasts as his girth swelled even larger.

Lily held him as the first jet fell like warm, wet lace over her nipples, and rolled her fist up and down his shaft as she leaned up and caught the second stream with her tongue. He put his hand over hers and painted her breasts and throat with his come.

Cadeyrn braced himself beside her, his breath warming her cheek as he rubbed his hand over her wet breasts. Lily caressed herself between her thighs, and then brought her slick fingers to his chest to paint her name on him. She knew without asking that neither of them would wash it away just yet. It was a little barbaric to brand him so, and to wear his seed like some exotic perfume, but it was also a deeply, wildly sexy secret.

He pressed her against him so that her breasts flattened against his chest, and the delicious scent of their pleasures blended to an erotic musk. He leaned in to kiss her eyelids shut, and held her that way until she started to doze.

They might not have spoken a word to each other, Lily thought as she gave up fighting against sleep, but they'd understood each other perfectly. She'd never known this, but she knew what it was. She'd wished on stars for it, and ached in her loneliness over it, and found her way to freedom in search of it.

Love.

Chapter Seventeen

F AR BEYOND THE mill to the west, Aon surfaced and surveyed the surrounding land. No sign of the Skaraven or the druidesses stolen from the mill appeared. To be sure the escaped were not hiding nearby, Aon released his seeker volatiles, which brought back nothing but the taste of sheep and ordinary mortals.

As the others came out of the ground he felt their hunger for mortal blood misting the air. They had not killed anything since the attack on the village, and soon the lust would make them crazed. Aon had no intention of being trapped in another henge because he could not control his urges, but he had the strength the others did not.

"They havenae come here," Ochd said as he shook off the earth and came to Aon. "We must go back."

"No' before we take them," Coig said, and jerked his hand at a large flock a half-league from them. "Look, many. I want them."

Tri's scarred face turned. "Hendry no' say kill meat."

"He doesnae mean the sheep." Ochd studied the mortal shepherds trying to herd their flock away from the giants. "There are but six."

"You speak like mortals," Coig sneered. "It makes my gullet fill."

Ochd smiled. "Like Lily? 'Tis a shame. You shall never have her as the Skaraven does."

"We dinnae come for shepherds," Aon told Coig. "We go back, search north." To Dha he said, "Take Tri. Find the Wood Dream. Move them to next place."

"I say stay," Coig said, and shoved Aon.

The others fell silent and moved back as they watched Coig's body release an attack mist.

Aon neutralized it with his own volatiles, but not before it wafted over Dha and Tri, who lunged at each other before staggering back as Aon shoved them apart.

"I am first," he told Coig. "I say what we do. We cannae lose the females."

"We dinnae need them," the sadistic giant said. "The Wood Dream female goes mad. Hendry does naught. We leave them, we do as we want."

The thought of abandoning the Wood Dream made Aon's own anger build. Coig had lost his connection to the lovers, but the rest of them remained their loyal guardians. The sadistic giant had become more trouble than he was worth, and soon Aon would have to do something about it. For now, he had to keep the peace.

"You take Lily when we find," Aon promised him. "She shall be yours to kill."

"To do as I wish first?" Coig asked, his hands rubbing together. "All I wish?"

"Aye," Aon agreed. Hendry would be angry with him, but he knew a clash among the giants would be worse. "When we take

them back, have Lily. Toy with her before you
snap her neck again. Kill the Skaraven."

"No," Coig said. "He lives. He watches me
have her."

Chapter Eighteen

⚜

CADEYRN OPENED HIS eyes to a deeper darkness, and heard soft noises coming from the hall. He looked down to see Lily sprawled across his belly, her beautiful face curtained by her hair. The moment he tried to shift her to his side, her hand came up to touch his face. He kissed the warm hollow of her palm.

"I don't want to move," she murmured, but she did, pushing herself up and yawning. "I think we should stay here and grow old together. Right in this bed." She smiled as she dipped her head and pressed her lips to his.

He would never tire of kissing Lily, Cadeyrn decided. When she would have ended it, he wrapped his arms around her, holding her against him as her warmth sank into his flesh. She felt as much a part of him now as his limbs, and more so. She had seen him, his true self, and she had freed him from the prison of his own making.

Lily drew back enough to study his face. "You look different. You're not happy, are you? Where is that glower I've come to fancy so much?"

Cadeyrn pretended to think. "Mayhap you have made me so. Or I may yet be drowsy and unable to muster a proper glower."

"I really like the glowering." She pursed her lips. "Then there's the scowling, the stern-eyed frown, the impatient glare. Oh, and that hooded look you give me when you think about shagging me. Like now."

"I shall hood my looks always," he promised. "If you will smile upon me when you think of shagging."

Lily smiled slowly.

Cadeyrn kissed her again and tucked her head against his shoulder. His battle spirit had brought them together to mate, but it had been her courage and determination that had breeched his heart and torn down his walls.

Now he understood fully what Brennus had found with his Althea: a trust so precious and all-consuming it had altered him forever.

Yet Lily had spoken of growing old together, when he could never do that now. Would she stay with him as he was, unchanging and eternal, while she lived out a mortal life?

"'Tis so much I must say to you." He cupped her jaw with his hand, and traced the curve of her bottom lip with his thumb. "But we've no time for talk—or shagging."

"We'll have plenty of both at Dun Mor, when you make me your bed-slave." She caught his thumb and nipped it before she sighed. "Now let me get dressed, boyo, before I start smiling again."

Cadeyrn nodded and climbed out of the bed to collect their garments.

Once dressed, they walked out to find Emeline and the sisters preparing a cold meal of bread, cheese and dried apple slices. The nurse darted a wide-eyed look at Lily before she blushed and limped into the kitchen.

"Evening, lovebirds," Rowan drawled as she offered them cups brimming with cider.

"It's hard, by the way." She glanced at the kitchen. "Florence had *two* cups."

Lily tasted it and sighed. "It's not a lukewarm toddy, but it'll do. Excuse me."

Cadeyrn watched her disappear into the kitchen before he regarded the sisters. "Have we offended Lady Emeline?"

"Ah, no." Rowan exchanged an amused look with Perrin. "Since she's as pure as Snow White before she met Le Prince, I actually think you've enlightened her."

"Oh, yeah," her sister said, nodding. "Last night was definitely an education."

"I'm no' catching the jest," he admitted.

"Emeline is our touchy-feely sponge," the carpenter told him. "She soaks up whatever emotions we're experiencing, usually when we're in close quarters. Anything we're feeling, like pain, nausea, fear...and the good stuff, too."

"If the feelings are strong enough, she can sense them from across a distance," Perrin added. "Like all the way from the master bed chamber to the back of the kitchen last night."

He finally understood what they were trying so hard not to say. "Fack me."

"Uh-uh-uh," Rowan said and shook a finger at him. "You two did enough of that last night."

"Grow up," Perrin told her sister, and then wrinkled her nose. "Cade, it's just that Emeline was right there with you and Lily. Emotionally speaking, I mean."

Lily and the nurse came out of the kitchen, and when Emeline saw how they looked at her she tossed up her hands.

"Stop gaping at me as if I'm on the mooch. I cannae help it." She turned to him. "I'm sorry, lad, truly I am. I'll try no' to intrude on your privacy again."

"What she means is, next time, get a room," Rowan quipped. "In another galaxy far, far away from her."

"Right," Lily said, folding her arms. "Now that we've thoroughly dissected me, Cade and Emeline, I think we should eat and get on with it."

Cadeyrn ate his meal quickly, and left the ladies to go to the stables. He saddled the five horses he judged suitable for the long ride, and turned out the rest so they could graze freely. He rode the biggest mare out, leading the others by long lines, and tethered them outside the big cottage.

Lily emerged bundled in a woolen blanket she'd folded and belted around her like a coat. The other lasses followed, each wearing several layers of garments against the cold. Like Lily they'd also donned boots, and Emeline had tied two thick splints of wood around one of her ankles.

"I've never ridden, of course," the nurse said. "I dinnae think I've done anything that suits this time except bleed." She inspected the mounts and squared her shoulders before she marched up to a broad-backed plow horse. "You look sturdy enough for me, lad." The gelding sniffed her hair and tried to chew on her braid. "On second thought, I think you're more suited to Rowan." Emeline tucked her braid inside her cloak and moved on to an older roan gelding that Cadeyrn had found still saddled. The horse checked her hands before it shuffled around to present its side to her in an obvious invitation. "And you already like me. Cade, if you could help me up into this contraption."

Lily watched Rowan help Perrin into the

saddle of a pretty chestnut before she expertly mounted the plow horse. That left a young white stallion for Lily, who took a moment to let him nuzzle her before she nodded to Cadeyrn, who lifted her up so she could swing her leg over his back. He let her settle herself for a moment before he spoke to them all.

"We ride north, toward the ridges on the horizon, where water may flow in the valleys. Take the same positions we used coming from the fortlet," Cadeyrn told them. "Take a better grip on the reins, Lady Emeline. That's the manner of it. If you see any sign of the *famhairean*, whistle like so." He let out a soft, three-note bird call.

Lily and the other ladies answered him with the same whistle.

"I would ride into battle with all of you," he praised them. "When we reach the forest at the base of the ridges we'll stop to rest the horses." He shifted his gaze to Emeline. "I ken you're yet weary, and wish it could be sooner, but we must cover as much ground as we may before moonrise."

"We'll keep up," the nurse promised, her expression resolute.

As soon as they rode out of the village the freezing night wind swept over them. The horses picked up their pace as they saw the wide stretch of land before them, but after the first league they slowed and glanced back at the village.

"They've never been taken out past the crop fields," Cadeyrn told Lily, and glanced back at the other ladies. "Keep their heads up, but dinnae jerk on the reins."

Emeline's roan squealed in response, as if to scold him for taking them from the only home they'd ever known.

"None of that," the nurse told the gelding, and stroked a hand along its neck. "We're going to the forest. Just think, you'll be warmer there out of the wind."

As if soothed by her touch and her voice, the gelding whickered low and settled back into a steady trot.

Another hour passed before they rode close enough to the forest for Cadeyrn to make out a glittering patch in the very center. He called on his battle spirit to aid his vision, which narrowed and extended over the distance they yet had to cross. The glitter came from a high, narrow waterfall that had not entirely frozen over. Beneath it he saw a small, dark pool that frothed beneath the cascade.

"There," he said to Lily, pointing to the falls before he turned his mount to face the others. "I see water ahead." He glanced at his lover. "'Tis our next ride, my lady."

Her gaze shifted past his shoulder, and her face went white. "Cade." She pointed back toward the village.

He turned to see a distant blur stretching out behind the cottages like a cloud rolling over the land. The air above the long, low mass filled with fountains of earth and rock as huge mounds of displaced soil rose and collapsed. One of the outlying cottages burst apart, collapsing into a heap.

The horses would never outrun the *famhairean*.

"Dismount," he told the others as he jumped down and swung Lily off her stallion. "Rowan."

"On it." The carpenter reached up to grab Emeline, easing her down. "But shouldn't we be riding like hell for the trees?"

"They'll follow the sound of the horses."
Cadeyrn slapped the horses on their flanks,
sending them galloping off. "While we'll run
there." He pointed to a section of the forest to
the east of the water. "Once in the trees we'll
head northwest and come up behind the falls.
You must keep hands on me when we go into
the pool, or I cannae bring you with me."

Rowan eyed her sister, who nodded as the
carpenter went to Emeline. "Want to be my
race buddy, Florence?" she asked as she
slipped her arm around the nurse's waist.

"Just keep me upright," Emeline told her.

Cadeyrn took hold of Perrin's and Lily's
hands before they set off. He kept their pace as
slow as he dared, glancing back frequently to
check the advancing *famhairean*. When he saw
that they wouldn't make the trees unless they
ran faster, he halted for a moment to hoist
Perrin to ride on his back while Rowan did the
same with the nurse.

"I'm jolly good," Lily said, panting the
words, but she didn't falter as they hurried for
the forest.

The furrows of earth shot away from them

as the giants followed the horses to the very edge of the trees. Just as they exploded out of the soil, Cadeyrn reached the forest. He ducked behind a large trunk, signaling for Rowan to do the same. Lily came around him and pressed against his front, while Perrin slid down from his back and braced herself against the big elm.

To the west, trees began falling and crashing to the ground as the giants marched into the forest.

Cadeyrn gestured for Rowan and Emeline to come to him. "Follow my steps and stay close. If you see anything coming toward us, hide yourselves."

The snow drifts carpeting the forest floor made it difficult to find safe footing, and Cadeyrn tamped down as much as he could as he gauged their position. He could hear and smell the falls but led his ladies deeper into the woods before he took a turn to the west. Something came hurrying toward them, and he dragged Lily and Emeline into the brush with him while Rowan and her sister disappeared.

Snow and ice covered the huge stag that

galloped past them, making his antlers and
hide look white.

Gods above, dinnae forsake us now.

Cadeyrn helped Lily and Perrin out of the
cover, and saw the sisters emerge from behind
a fallen oak. Rowan made a circle with her
thumb and forefinger before she boosted her
sister over the obstacle.

Two choices lay before him, Cadeyrn
thought as he scanned their surroundings. He
could find a place for them to hide and hope
to wait out the *famhairean*. But though the
darkness weakened them, that was no guar-
antee they would remain safe. He saw no caves
or hollows in the forest that would protect the
lasses from the cold and wind for the rest of
the night.

The alternative would prove even more
dangerous. He could have them gather the
dregs of their strength and make one last, bold
dash for the falls. The sound of a distant
rumble shivered through the air, and he felt
the earth beneath his feet tremble as if afraid
of it.

Lily gripped his hands and whispered,
"They've found us."

Chapter Nineteen

SEARCHING MADDOCK MCARA'S lands made Althea appreciate how well the laird treated his tenants. At every farm he stopped and dismounted to greet the wary-eyed farmers, and told them only that he'd brought most of his clansmen and the Skaraven to assure they were safe. He also knew all of their names and asked after their families. The wives brought out their babies for him to admire, while their husbands produced dark bottles of whiskey. The McAra took a swig at every farm but never seemed to get drunk.

"He must have an iron stomach," Althea murmured to Brennus as the laird bid farewell at their latest stop.

"The tribe of Ara were near weaned on *uisge beatha*, as I recall," the chieftain told her. In a lower voice he added, "Look closer when the wee laird takes the bottle. He holds his arm before his throat, to hide that it doesnae move with a swallow."

"He's faking it?" Althea chuckled when Brennus nodded. "So he doesn't insult the farmers while he avoids getting plastered." As the laird mounted and rode up to join them, she smiled and said, "I think your name should be McShrewd, my lord."

"Och, but I'm a simple man, my lady." Maddock waved to the farmers and winked at her. "And one who well kens his lack of weight."

At their next stop one of the tenants apologized to the laird for not sending the wheat and barley flour that Maddock's steward had ordered.

"I sent me grain to the mill as soon as we harvested, but word's come the water's dried up, milord," the farmer said.

Maddock exchanged a look with Brennus before he clapped the farmer on the shoulder.

"There'll be no grinding without water. We'll attend to this directly."

Brennus made a circling gesture with his hand before gesturing forward, and once the laird rejoined them they rode to a nearby glen. There the laird and the chieftain dismounted, and consulted Maddock's map before Brennus addressed the men.

"We'll ride first to the mill. My men will approach, so you'll have our backs," he told the McAra clansmen. "Maddock, if we engage the *famhairean*, you'll collect the people still living and get them away."

"Stay behind the Skaravens' swords," Kanyth added, and dragged a dirk over his palm, holding it up to show the wound before he poured water from a flask over it. He lifted his hand again so the McAra clansmen could watch the gash close and vanish. "We're no' as easy to kill."

"If you're wounded," Taran said, his quiet voice sounding loud in the shocked stillness, "clasp your arms around your mount's neck. I'll send it and you out of harm's way."

"You cannae control our horses, man," a big clansman riding a massive destrier said.

"Actually, he can," Althea advised him.

Taran crooked his finger at the war horse, which hurried over to him without hesitation. The horse master pointed to the ground, and the massive animal dropped down, shaking off the clansman before rolling away from him and pawing the air with his hooves.

The big man stood and stared down at his mount before eyeing Taran. "Could you do that with a lass?"

"Why? You cannae coax one to your bed with your charms?" Taran countered, making the other men chuckle.

"You've seen what we can do, so use us as your shields," Brennus said. He looked around at the laird's men. "The giants have unmatchable strength, and cannae be killed. Dinnae attack them. If they come at you, cut off their arms and then their legs. 'Tis the only method to hamper the bastarts." He turned to regard Althea. "My lady wife—"

"—is perfectly capable of defending herself," she reminded him, and dismounted to walk over to a large shrub. She touched it, pouring her ice power into it, and then stood back to let the men see its whitened, frozen glitter. She flicked a finger against it, making it shatter and fall into a heap of broken crystals. "I can do the same to the *famhairean*."

Maddock walked over to inspect the remains of the shrub before meeting her gaze. "By the Gods. What need we swords when we have you, my lady?"

"Because there's only *one* of me, and *lots* of them." Althea glanced at the stunned faces around them. "Best to stay clear of my hands in battle, too, lads."

The men collectively murmured ayes, and a few inched away from her.

From there they rode in battle formation toward the mill, and stopped a short distance away to survey the surrounding land.

"I see smoke." Althea pointed to a haze lingering just above the trees.

"More on the wind," Brennus said and breathed in. "'Tis no' from a hearth. Kanyth, Taran, with me." The three men jumped to the ground and in moments had disappeared into the trees.

Althea wanted to go with them but knew someone had to defend McAra and his clans-men. But as the minutes passed, and the longer they were gone, the tighter she gripped her mount's reins.

"Have faith, my lady," Maddock murmured to her.

"I'd have more at his side," she admitted, and then saw three shadows separating from the trees. "There they are."

"They've abandoned the place," Brennus said as he came to lift her down from the horse. "Set fire to the mill house as well, and 'tis smoldering. Come with me, Wife."

Brennus led her to a small out building, where she saw a huge stone wheel and a broken door by the entry. Inside the dark interior he lit a lamp to show her discarded garments. The women had been kept here. Althea turned around until she saw three stones sitting atop a wooden bin.

"They left a message," she said and went over and raised the lid. Words were scratched into the wood.

"Burned the mill. Escaped with Cade. R.E.L.P.'"

"What does relp mean?" Brennus asked.

"It's their initials. Rowan, Emeline, Lily

and Perrin." She met her husband's gaze. "They're all still alive."

"Then we may yet hope." He walked out to survey the area as the laird joined them.

"Some of them took a wagon to the east," Maddock said, gesturing to wheel ruts in the ground. "No' many, mayhap two or three." He nodded in the direction of the furrows crossing the fields, which went in the opposite direction. "The giants tunneled west."

Kanyth emerged from the trees and trotted over to them. "I've found passage markers in the woods," he told the chieftain. "They're Cade's. I'm sure of it."

"Laird McAra," Brennus said, "you and your men should follow the cart. Likely Hendry and Murdina took it to get away after the mill burned. We'll track our people and the *famhairean*. Dinnae try to capture the druids. Only follow them."

"Please be careful, my lord," Althea said. "Henry and Murdina have powerful abilities, and they won't hesitate to use them against you and your men."

"Aye, my lady," Maddock said and signaled to his clansmen to follow him. To Brennus he said, "May the Gods ride with you, Chieftain."

Brennus sent half of the Skaraven with Kanyth and Taran to follow the furrows west, and led the remainder with him and Althea into the forest. When she saw the oak grove portal that had been blocked by a heap of millstones anger welled up inside her. How like Hendry and Murdina to make sure that none of the women could open it and escape. Something on the ground caught her eye. She crouched to find a few strands of long blonde hair with dried blood holding them together.

"I think Lily might be hurt," she said, showing it to Brennus.

"Aye, and Cade carried her, for his boot marks grow deeper here." He surveyed the grove before eyeing a tree, and strode over to pluck some dead leaves stuck in its bark. "They came this way."

Althea noticed that while Cadeyrn had managed to conceal any trace of his passage Brennus seemed to have no difficulty tracking his path. "Where are these markers Kanyth said he found?"

"All around us." The chieftain stopped and

pointed to a pine branch with some bent needles, and a bunch of twigs on a patch of moss. "Five crooked needles. Five fallen twigs. On the tree, five leaves left wedged. Cade uses clan ciphers for his markers."

Althea eyed the moss. "What does five twigs mean?"

"He's four lasses with him," Brennus said as he looked away from her.

She tugged on his arm. "You're really a horrible liar. Tell me."

"Five isnae good. 'Tis our cipher for uncertainty." He hesitated before he said, "Five tells me he's no' sure he'll survive."

That meant the other women were at risk, and Althea wasn't going to waste another moment talking about it. "Well, then let's go and find our war master, Chieftain."

Cadeyrn's markers ended at the edge of the forest, but at the last Brennus crouched and brushed some leaves away from the soil. That revealed lines of rocks pressed into the ground. The irregular grid-like arrangement was parted down the middle. Brennus stood and looked north, as Althea followed his gaze.

"Are you seeing what I'm seeing?" she asked, awe in her voice.

"Aye," he said, nodding toward the hill.

In the distance stood a rocky hill that looked as if it had been split in half. Cadeyrn, the war master whose battle spirit was the sharp-sighted owl, had left this message. But so had Brennus's battle spirit when it had neatly cleaved a ghostly, gray owl down the middle in the stronghold's *caibeal*. Althea's heart beat a little faster, and the faintest hope stirred deep in her chest.

"He's taken them to the divide there," Brennus said. He turned to call to the men to mount up, and then helped Althea onto her horse. "We must ride swiftly now."

She patted her mare before she gathered the reins. "We're ready."

Loping across the fields toward the crevasse, Althea silently prayed that they'd find Brennus's second and the women hiding there. Once they reached the base of the huge crack, however, Brennus dismounted to find another coded message left in stones that told them Cadeyrn and the women had moved on to a nearby village.

"We're going to end up following them all the way back to Dun Mor," she grumbled, as Brennus climbed up on his mount.

The chieftain wasted no time as he led the troop directly across a dry river bed.

"Is this the river that Hendry dammed so you couldn't approach by water?"

"Aye," he said. "But no' only that. Hendry needs to protect the giants. Water makes them revert to their old forms."

"You mean, it turns them back into trees?" When he nodded Althea glanced up at the sky. "When can we expect the next rainstorm?"

"After the thaw, in six moons," Brennus said sounding grim now. "If winter lingers, mayhap seven. Come, Wife."

Before they reached the village Brennus spotted new furrows of displaced earth streaking in from the west. He signaled for the men to change formation, and the Skaraven moved themselves into a tight defensive ring around Althea and her mate. Seeing the cottages that had been destroyed made her stomach clench, and then Brennus shifted position in front of her.

"I can't see through you," she told him,

and then realized why that was. She swallowed against her tight throat before she asked, "Are they all dead?"

"I cannae say from this distance, lass," he admitted. "But the pond behind the shearing house, 'tis full of bodies."

"Check the pond and the village," he ordered some of the men. "Lively now, lads."

Manath signaled to a small group and galloped off as they followed.

"Damn them," Althea said, her throat tight. She wiped at her stinging eyes, and then found herself being plucked from her saddle and cradled in her husband's strong arms. "They were so close to coming home."

"Cade would have used the pond if he could," Brennus said. He frowned and looked over at it. "Even injured, the water would have healed him."

Althea pressed the heels of her hands against her stinging eyes. "Please, God."

The men galloped back to report that the pond had been frozen after the bodies were dumped in it, and they'd seen only the remains of villagers there. They'd also discovered that someone had occupied the largest of the cottages as recently as that morning.

"Chieftain, these I took from the trash," Manath said, and showed him a pair of badly worn shoes with blackened steel toes.

"Lily's shoes," Althea said. She reached for them, not caring that they covered her hands with dirt. "She hated them so much she would have ditched them as soon as she found something else to wear." She smiled at her husband. "They're alive. I know it."

Ailpin pointed past the collapsed cottages. "I reckon they may yet be, my lady," he said. "More sign of the *famhairean* go from here toward the ridges. They may yet pursue our war master."

"Then we ride to the ridges after them," Brennus said. "Quickly."

Chapter Twenty

✥✥✥

L ILY HURRIED AFTER Cadeyrn as he led them deeper into the forest, away from the approaching force. Twilight had deepened into nightfall, but the moon shed enough light to help them avoid the worst of the obstacles. When she glanced over her shoulder to check on the others she saw Rowan helping a badly-limping Emeline, and Perrin lagging behind them.

"I'll get her," she told her lover. "We need you in the lead." Dropping back, she put her arm around the dancer. "Lean on me, sweetheart."

"I'm fine," Perrin whispered as she did just that. "Lily, they're too close now. Cade won't be able to reach the waterfall unless we create a diversion."

"Yes, he will. We're going to keep running," she told her firmly as she hauled her through a tangle of branches. A strange surge of icy heat ran down the length of her arms. "Don't give up now, Perrin."

"I can't see it," the other woman said. "When I think of the water and Dun More all I see is a desert, and a golden castle. Empty, bleeding eye sockets carved into the walls. It's awful."

Lily tripped over her own feet and nearly fell. "Sorry. It's just your mind playing tricks on you again. There aren't any castles out here."

"This one was in Cade's chest," Perrin insisted, her voice wavering. "And someone had chopped off his head."

"Right," Lily said. If Perrin kept talking like this Lily would be sick all over both of them. She also knew that Perrin's visions didn't always come true. "What sort of diversion can we make, then?"

"When we see the falls, I'll break off and

run the other way," Perrin told her. "You get everyone into the water and go with Cade."

"And leave you behind to die?" She almost slapped her. "After we've done all this bloody work to get away? I'd kill you myself first."

"They won't." The dancer grinned. "They need one of us to open the portals for them. I'll be the only future druid left. Hendry will have no choice but to protect me. Once you're safe, you come back for me, okay? And bring lots of those lovely Scottish highlanders with you."

Lily suddenly knew the other woman wasn't telling her the whole truth. The details of the vision of the castle were ghastly correct. There had to be more to it. Why would Perrin want to sacrifice herself now, when they were so close to freedom?

"Please, Lily," Perrin pleaded, sounding almost tearful. "I went along with your scheme to get Cade here. It's my turn to play Druid Roulette."

She could feel the knobby bones of the dancer's spine poking into the arm that supported her. Perrin had grown so thin and weak she had to be running by pure stubborn will alone. When Coig found them all gone, he wouldn't cradle the dancer in his massive arms and croon sweet things to her. No, he'd grab her by the neck and drag her back to Hendry and Murdina—and deliver her limp and lifeless.

If traveling through the portal hadn't healed her, that would have been Lily's fate.

Her arms burned, and this time Lily could feel the outline of every feather scarred into her skin. More than the sensation, she felt the presence of something inside her that reminded her of what she felt whenever she touched Cadeyrn's ink. Until that moment she hadn't really believed it was some battle spirit, but it flooded her now with the same strength she'd used to walk out of her father's mansion.

What shall you give for my warrior?

My heart. My life.

Lily had made so few choices in her life that she knew how important they could be. She'd chosen to go into therapy, and leave Edgar, and begin a new life as a cruise ship sous-chef. That had changed her destiny. She'd chosen Cadeyrn to be her lover and her love, and she'd gone into his heart to free him from his fortress of loneliness. That had filled the emptiness in her own battered soul. She'd lived a lifetime of happiness in only a few days after a short life filled with endless fear and misery. Lily desperately wanted more time, time to love and to be loved. But to save the man who had saved her, and the women who had become her sisters, it would have to be enough.

"What do you say?" the dancer asked. "Will you help me?"

"Yes, Perrin, I will," she said, not meaning a word of it as she used her power to pick up a good-sized rock and drop it firmly on the back of the other woman's neck.

The dancer's eyes rolled up in her head, and she sagged against Lily. Taking a firm grip on her, she held her against her side just as Cadeyrn fell back to join them.

"Too much exercise for her, I think," Lily said, as he picked up the unconscious woman. "Just before she blacked out she had one of her visions. She told me that we must run for the falls right this minute, or we won't make it."

"You're sure?" he asked as Rowan and Emeline joined them.

I love him, Lily thought, amazed by how powerful that made her. "Absolutely, boyo. Now which way is it?"

As soon as Cadeyrn nodded to the west they headed in that direction, plowing through snowy brush and weaving through a labyrinth of pine and alder. Branches clawed at Lily, and one time she skidded on a patch of hard-crusted snow and nearly smacked face-first into a tree trunk. But she soon heard the sound of rushing water as the ground sloped upward, and went to help Rowan climb with Emeline wedged between them.

"Tell me this will be the last of it," the nurse panted, her face so pale now it looked like a plaster mask. "Lie to me if you must."

"Don't sweat it, Florence," Rowan told her. "We're almost there."

Lily heard something snap, and then Emeline uttered a low cry.

"What was that?" Lily gasped.

"Never mind it." The nurse gripped her more tightly. "Just dinnae let go of me, or I'll slide down this slope like a bloody avalanche."

Rowan braced her shoulder under Emeline's arm. "Then you're taking me with you."

They emerged from the trees onto a rocky cliff with high, jagged boulders gating the mountain stream that powered the falls. Lily could see the boulders were too high and steep to climb over to get to the water. Cadeyrn eased Perrin down to the ground before he went with Lily to the edge to look down. Beneath them a pool of dark water churned. He looked back at the other women.

"'Tis too far for them to jump," he said, and looked up at the boulders. "We must climb a little higher to get into the stream."

"More climbing." Emeline muffled a groan as she collapsed onto the ground. "Could you give us a moment, lad? I think my ankle's broken."

"Okay," Rowan said, breathing hard. "There's a big lump on the back of my sister's head." She glared at Lily. "Like someone bashed her with a rock. Again."

"She was going to try something ridiculous," Lily assured her. "Since you always chase after her when she does, you'd both be killed. I'll apologize as soon as she wakes up."

"Next time," Rowan said, "just give me the rock."

All around the base of the falls the ground began to undulate and crumble, and several small trees made an eerie sound as they uprooted and fell over to crash into the brush. The disturbance flushed animals from the surrounding woods to run or fly away. Then the air went still.

"The bastarts have tracked us," Cadeyrn said, his hands fisting.

Emeline tried to stand, staggered and fell on all fours. "Do you reckon I could crawl to higher ground? I'm a good crawler."

"I'll carry you, Florence." Rowan brought Perrin over to Cade. "If you can handle two."

"One, actually," Lily said as she stepped to the very edge of the cliff. "Get to climbing. I'll hold them off for as long as I can."

"Are you out of your mind?" the carpenter demanded. "It's six stories down. Get away from there."

"Take our ladies to higher ground and get them to Dun Mor, right away," Lily told

Cadeyrn, who was putting Perrin's limp form back on the ground. When he met her gaze, she smiled. "I love you, boyo. Never forget that."

"Gods, Lily." As he started toward her his expression filled with something she had never seen him once show: fear. "You cannae do this."

"Terribly sorry, love. My choice, really."

She turned and spread her arms as she jumped off the cliff.

Falling was almost as exhilarating as flying, Lily thought as she plummeted. She turned slowly, letting the air stream over her, and felt as free as she did in Cadeyrn's arms.

She hit the water a moment after she heard her lover shout her name, and the shock of the icy pool knocked the breath from her lungs. Falling might be lovely, but drowning was decidedly not. Kicking madly, she surfaced, gasping for air. Her back and legs ached from the impact, but the water almost instantly numbed them. She shook the wet hair from her face as the *famhairean* began clawing their way out of the earth.

"Lily," Cadeyrn shouted from above.

"Hello, you sodding monsters," she called out, grinning at their hate-filled cracked faces. "Did you enjoy scampering about the countryside? Not that you could scamper. You lot are nothing but oversized worms."

Coig uttered a scratchy, horrible sound as he trudged toward the pool. "Come to me, you conniving mortal snail. Come now and I willnae pull off your arms and stuff them down your deceitful throat."

"You had your chance, you sadistic wanker."

She swam backward as she summoned all of her power and directed it at the first pair that came out of the ground. Her push sent them flying into another pair while she redirected her power to the water around her. It rose up like a shimmering curtain to surround the pool with a ten-foot wall.

"Get out of there, you ditz," Rowan yelled down to her. "Run while you still can."

"Busy," Lily called back.

Pain blossomed behind her eyes. When she wiped a warm trickle from her nose, blood flowered over her knuckles.

"Lily, for the love of the Gods." That was

Cadeyrn, and he sounded as if he might jump off the cliff now.

"I'm all right here, my lover," she said as she looked up at him. "But I can't hold this forever."

Something hit the water with a splash and zipped past her. Lily felt a slice of pain across her outer arm. The freezing water around her took on a scarlet tinge as she ducked another spear that came hurtling at her head. More followed, some piercing the depths around her while others flew up over her toward the top of the falls. She heard Rowan cry out, and then Cadeyrn shouting for the women to take cover.

It would all be for nothing unless she stopped the spears as well as the giants.

Something hot and agonizing pounded from inside Lily's skull as she poured on more power to hurl back the weapons. Only a few got past her, but when she heard Emeline shriek in pain, she knew she'd have to go full on with everything she had. With a huge mental shove, she sent the wall of water directly at the *famhairean*, dousing all of them.

The giants' sodden bodies shook as twigs

and leaves sprouted all over them. Coig, who got the worst of the soaking, suddenly grew roots that sank deep into the ground. When he met her gaze, he looked exactly as Edgar had when he'd gotten a quail so stuffed with dill it reeked like a giant sour pickle.

Good-bye, Daddy.

As much pain as she was in, seeing Coig rendered immobile made laughter pour out of Lily.

"I win, Coig, you gormless manky plonker."

Her pleasure didn't last too long. A few moments later her vision dimmed, and her left arm became completely useless. She couldn't move her left leg, either, so her body began to sink.

Emeline had warned her about this.

Brilliant. I've had a stroke.

As the frigid water closed over her pounding head, she looked up through the bubbling water to see a transparent shape splash down into the depths. Suddenly cool blue light enveloped her, wrapping her in the softest sensation, as if she were being cradled by downy wings.

The shape turned dark, and then became Cadeyrn.

Hard hands seized her, and water rushed around her. Her lover swam with her to the surface, water streaming down his face as he held her plastered against his chest.

"I willnae let you go," he said, his voice shaking. "You must stay with me and love me, lass, for that is your punishment. I shall marry you to be sure of it."

She couldn't speak. Her mouth moved but only slurred sounds came out of it. Somehow, she dragged up the one arm that still worked, and put her hand to his face. She could hear more giants coming up out of the ground, and the cries of the wounded women at the top of the falls. She closed her eyes, calling on Cadeyrn's battle spirit to help her, and with the last of her strength pushed him away.

Do your job now, my love. Save our ladies. Save yourself.

Chapter Twenty-One

❧❀❧

CADEYRN DRAGGED LILY to him yet again, and saw the blood trickling from her nose and ears. He gripped her neck and moved his fingers until he found her pulse, which throbbed slow and weak. Half of her face had pulled down, distorting her pretty features. He couldn't leave her, but with the advancing *famhairean* he couldn't carry her up to the other lasses.

Gods, that you would thrust this choice upon me.

At the top of the falls he saw Rowan with a hand to her blood-soaked shoulder. Emeline clutched her side with both hands but blood seeped through her fingers. Perrin still lay unconscious where he had put her. The three of them couldn't climb down to him. With such injuries either or both might soon bleed out.

Cadeyrn would not sacrifice the other lasses to save his dying love. Nor could he leave Lily behind to die alone. They would have to do as he did.

"Rowan," he shouted, and when the carpenter looked down at him he pointed to the cliff's edge. "Jump. All of you."

"You're insane," she called back.

"Lily survived," he shouted. "So can you."

Just then a spear whizzed by so close that it nearly parted her hair. She hoisted Perrin over her unwounded shoulder and held her hand out to Emeline, who shook her head. Rowan said something to her and held out her arm. When the nurse hobbled over to her, Rowan clamped her against her side.

Emeline let out a screech as Rowan jumped over the edge with her and Perrin.

They fell in the water with a tremendous splash. Cadeyrn held onto Lily as he swam one-armed over toward the other women. Spears began shooting past him, and then he heard a voice bellow in the old tongue.

"Bràithrean an fhithich."

He turned his head to see his chieftain and clan ride in behind the giants, their swords flashing in the moonlight as they hacked away the *famhairean's* limbs. Beside Brennus his wife also rode, her pale slender hands freezing every giant she touched.

The Gods *had* heard him, and had answered in the best possible manner.

Cadeyrn reached for Rowan, tugging her and the other lasses to him as he took on his water-traveling form. "Keep hold of me."

"You got it, pal."

The carpenter wrapped one arm around his neck, and used her other hand to cover Perrin's nose and mouth. Emeline grasped him around the waist.

At long last he sank down into the icy waters, filling them with bubbling light as he envisioned the river outside Dun Mor, and streamed from the waterfall into the currents that transported him and his ladies to the other side of the highlands. When he surfaced and returned to his human form, Rowan released him and looked around at the Great Wood.

"You really were telling the truth." She

chuckled and shook her head as she dragged Perrin and Emeline over to the bank. "Come on, Florence. We're safe now."

As soon as Cadeyrn released her, Emeline helped Rowan shift Perrin onto the bank. Then she turned around and slapped the carpenter with a loud, cracking blow.

"That's for dragging me over the cliff," Emeline said flatly. "I told you I'm terrified of heights. I cannae swim, either. And I might have bled to death." When Rowan opened her mouth, she held up her hand. "If you call me Florence again, you hateful wench, I'll break your pretty nose."

"Duly noted. By the way, I'm really sorry I didn't leave you to die." The carpenter rubbed her cheek as she watched Cadeyrn carry Lily out of the currents. "What's wrong with her face?"

The nurse glanced at Lily, made a sharp noise and limped and hopped down to join them.

"Put her on the ground, please, lad." When he did she pushed up Lily's eyelids and checked her ears. "Lily? Can you hear me?"

At that moment Perrin's eyes opened, and

she rubbed the back of her head. "Why am I wet? I was talking to Lily. Oh, my God." She sat up and looked around them. "Ro?"

"She knocked you out," her sister said, crouching down to give her a hug. "You missed the spear and water fight, too." Her dark eyes met Cadeyrn's gaze. "Lily and our Skaraven saved us."

He held onto his lover's hand. *Now you must save me, my lady.*

"Cade, it looks as if she's had a stroke," Emeline said very gently. When she saw his blank look she added, "The blood to her brain was cut off, likely when she used too much power. It causes paralysis on one side of the body."

He told himself she still breathed, and her heart still beat. Death had not snatched her from him…yet.

"Can she recover from it, Emeline?"

"Some do, but the damage is done," she told him. "We need to get her inside and warm."

"Mayhap I can be of aid," a deep voice rumbled as a huge shape stepped out of the shadows.

Perrin screamed and lunged in front of her sister.

"It's okay, Perr," Rowan said and patted her back as she regarded Ruadri. "Just FYI, we're not good with sneaky, supersize guys appearing out of thin air. Cade?"

"'Tis our clan's shaman, Ruadri." He tried to focus on his brother, but his mind still reeled with what the nurse had said. "He's the most trusted of my brothers, so dinnae fear him."

The shaman carefully approached, while the nurse hopped backward and put more space between her and Ruadri.

"My lady," the shaman said, sounding pained. "I shallnae harm you. I'm a healer, like you."

"You just stay away from me," Emeline told him, sounding furious now.

"Ru, summon the sentries and take the lasses back to the stronghold." Cadeyrn lifted Lily and carried her to him. As he handed her to his brother it felt as if he were wrenching off his arms. "She used too much of her power, and 'tis made her apoplectic. I must borrow your blade and return to the battle."

Ruadri turned to one side so Cadeyrn

could draw his sword from his belt. "I'll do what I can for her and see her safe until your return."

"Go carefully, Brother. She's my heart."

Cadeyrn kissed Lily's brow before he turned and ran to the river. He dove in without looking back. Bonding with the water, he raced back to the ridge falls and emerged from the pool with Ruadri's blade in his hand and wrath in his heart.

Brennus and the clan had moved into a long, rectangular schiltron formation to create a living wall around the *famhairean* and block the escape of those not yet sprouting branches. Most of the giants had their backs to the water, giving Cadeyrn the advantage of approaching them unseen. His hands gripped the hilt of the long sword, finding the proper hold as he came upon them from behind. He struck two with a forward and back blow, sending pieces of them flying as he sliced off the arms in which they held spears. As they tottered, he cut their legs out from under them.

Another turned to jab a spear at him, hatred in his face.

Cadeyrn caught the weapon and wrenched it out of the giant's hands. "You dinnae fight unarmed lasses now, you cowardly *cac*."

Kicking the *famhair's* knee broke its leg, and with a savage thrust he drove his sword through its neck. With a twist of his hands he decapitated the giant and shoved aside the headless torso to ram the stolen spear into the face of the next to rush him. He quickly surveyed the battle. Lady Althea moved among the fallen *famhairean* using her freezing power to make sure they'd never rise. Cadeyrn noted the positions of his clan and the giants still able to fight. They had clustered tightly, the weakness of the untrained.

"Brennus," he shouted to the chieftain. "Thistle bloom."

The chieftain called out the maneuver. The Skaraven shifted into a tight inverted triangle, their blades pointed outward in a continuous fan of lethal iron. With a flurry of chops, thrusts, and great arcing swings of his blade, Cadeyrn drove the *famhairean* before him and around the triangle. Instantly the formation spread out like a blooming thistle, surging past the confused giants, before the men reversed direction and trapped their enemy within it.

Limbs and spears flew into the air, until one of the giants called out, "To the Wood Dream."

Cadeyrn roared his fury as he shouldered past his brothers to see the giants disappear into the ground. Glaring yellow lights rose from the injured to plunge after them. Huge furrows knocked the Skaraven from their feet. But Cadeyrn stabbed at the earth, hacking deep until a hard hand jerked him upright.

"They've fled," Brennus told him, and nodded past his shoulder. "All but that one."

Cadeyrn turned to see the *famhair* that Lily had called Coig, the one she most hated, the one that had broken her neck. The water had left him rooted fast by the edge of the pool, his form distorted by a growing tangle of ugly limbs. Cadeyrn stalked over and around to behold the giant's face still visible in the tumorous growth.

"You cannae kill us, you mindless fool," Coig said, his grating voice filled with gloating satisfaction. "My kin shall fashion a new form for me, and I'll have her again. When I do I'll fack her with my great hard—"

Cadeyrn drove his blade into the giant's mouth, splintering the remains of his teeth and slicing down deep to silence his tongue. He drew back his sword to hack at the branches and outgrowths, over and again, until Coig mutely stared out of a ragged stump. He then called to his clan, and they gathered around the giant.

"For my lady, that you may never touch another innocent again."

Cadeyrn hacked at the roots from under the stump. When he'd freed it from the ground the clan helped him lift and heave it into the water, where it sank to the bottom.

Brennus came to stand beside him and watched the churning surface. "It doesnae rise to take another form."

"'Tis as I reckoned," Cadeyrn told him tonelessly. "The true reason they avoid water. They cannae escape it. The tree-knowers should have put them in a facking loch."

"Aye." The chieftain squeezed his shoulder. "Now that we ken this, we've a powerful new weapon. Imagine the pit traps we might set."

Cadeyrn nodded, but the only thing that filled his head was handing over his lover to Ruadri and leaving her. He should have stayed. She could be dying this moment.

Althea appeared beside him and regarded the pool. "We should post a no-swimming sign here, I think. How are our girls?"

"Wounded, but yet strong," he told her, and then found himself in an affectionate embrace. "My lady, you should ken that Lily… She…"

"I saw what she did, and what it did to her." She drew back. "Don't give up on her yet. Lily's one very tough gal."

Shouts came from behind them, and Cadeyrn turned to see more Skaraven riding through the trees toward them. Kanyth dismounted and trotted quickly to take him in a rib-cracking hold as he pounded his back.

"I ken you to be too cunning to die, you great schemer." His grin vanished as he saw his face. "Never tell me you didnae save the lassies."

"He did," Brennus said before Cadeyrn could reply. "What of the giants?"

"They doubled back here." The weapons

master surveyed the ruins and remains of the battle. "And you couldnae wait for us to share in the glory, you selfish bastarts. Do you think I make blades for the art of it?"

"Certainly no' for the comfort," the chieftain said drily.

Taran rode up to the falls and dismounted, clasping forearms with Cadeyrn before he said to Brennus, "The new furrows subside at the treeline. They must have gone deeper to avoid our pursuing them beyond it."

"We've dealt them a heavy blow," Brennus declared. "'Twill take much time for them to fashion new bodies for the escaped. We'll join the McAra and see what they've learned." Brennus caressed his wife's face. "You should return to Dun Mor and see to our ladies."

"Yes, I think I've had enough glory for one day." She kissed his palm. "Cade, would you mind being my escort?"

Though Cadeyrn's heart ached for Lily, he waited for the chieftain.

Brennus nodded his agreement. "Go to her, lad. With our thanks."

Chapter Twenty-Two

B RENNUS RODE FROM the ridges with his clan to follow the trail of McAra, his mind much occupied with this new revelation about the *famhairean*. He also wondered if his second would ever be the same after his ordeal, and said as much to his weapons master.

"He'd best be," Kanyth told him. "Much as I've learned from serving in his place, being your second demands too much thinking. I've no' the head for it."

Taran rode up alongside them. "The horses smell their kin." He nodded at a grove a short distance ahead. "By the stream there." He sniffed the wind coming from that direction. "They're no' wounded."

That relieved Brennus, for he'd worried his mortal allies might try to capture the druids. "We'll water our mounts there while I speak to the laird."

When they reached the grove and dismounted, the McAra emerged looking quite sour.

"I wagered you'd have the pleasure of fighting the bastarts without us." Maddock inspected them before eyeing the chieftain. "I should start a clan war and have you ride at our backs. Only they'd run like lambs at the sight of you." He called for his men to help the Skaraven water their tired horses.

Brennus grunted. "And what of the druids?"

The laird's amusement evaporated. "We tracked their cart to a market town three leagues to the north. I had the men block every road out before we began a search. I felt sure we had them cornered in a drying shed. Just as we were to storm it the earth shook and swallowed it whole. I mused on following the furrows east, but your warning no' to brace them rang in my ears. You'll make a cowering lassie out of me soon, Chieftain."

"'Twas the prudent choice, Maddock." Brennus's respect for the little laird increased with every demonstration of his wisdom. "If by chance the McAra ever face a clan war, the Skaraven shall have your backs."

"If I didnae like McFarlan so much, I might attack him on the morrow." The McAra brushed something from his sleeve. "What now, then?"

"Cadeyrn, my second, discovered something after the battle that we didnae ken about the *famhairean*." Brennus explained what had happened to Coig after the rest of the giants escaped. "I must consult with the tree-knowers to be sure, but I reckon 'tis their greatest weakness. They've gone to much trouble to conceal it from us. 'Twill be the means to set a fine trap for the rest."

Maddock nodded. "Since the others ran before you tossed him in the water, they yet dinnae ken that you've got them by the baws. I'd take pains to conceal you've fathomed this. How may the McAra aid you?"

"I willnae have druids at Dun Mor," Brennus admitted. "My brothers wouldnae tolerate it, nor will my belly. You and I might

meet with Bhaltair Flen at your stronghold, if
you'd grant me the favor."

"Since I'm included, I'm happy to play
host." The laird rubbed his lower lip. "And
have my map maker begin searching his scrolls
for every deep loch that may serve your
purpose."

Brennus saw Taran watching them as if
waiting for a chance to approach, and excused
himself to consult with the horse master. "Are
the mounts ready for the jaunt back to
Dun Mor?"

"Aye, and I've checked their blinders." He
glanced at Maddock, who was speaking to two
of his chieftains. "There's a grand warrior
stuffed in that wee laird. He's fearless, and
noble of heart."

"'Twas a good choice to make the McAra
our allies," Brennus agreed, "but that isnae
why you watched us, Tran."

His horse master smiled a little. "I saw the
black-haired lass before Cade took her and the
others to Dun Mor. According to Lady Althea
she may share the McAra name and, I
suspect, the bloodline. She hasnae mentioned

her to the laird, but now that she's come to Dun Mor, word may reach him."

Brennus had given some thought to the implications of having one of Maddock's kin —distant as she was—under Skaraven protection.

"I know naught of the customs of this time," he said, "but I'll wager as blood-kin she's still clan."

In the time of the Pritani tribes young females had been highly prized, not only for their beauty but their fertility and talents. From what Brennus had seen of Clan McAra, the chieftains and high-ranking clansmen all had wives as lovely and shapely as Emeline. No doubt the laird had a hand in arranging or approving all the matches, just as the Pritani headmen once did.

"If she were a man, 'twould no' matter," Taran said softly. "But a comely lass with druid blood and healer training, 'tis quite another thing. I'll wager she's more valuable than a hundred of his finest mares."

"Aye, McAra would be a fool no' to claim her." Brennus felt the weight of the new dilemma like a thick cloak in high summer. "Fack me, but for every knot I unravel two more appear. What do you advise?"

"Say naught for the present to the laird," the horse master said, sounding wry. "Speak with your lady on the matter when we return to Dun Mor. We ken naught of the customs of her time. Then do as you ever would: what 'tis best for all."

Kanyth came over with a bottle of whiskey. "I favor our mortal allies. They carry drink with them into battle." He took a swallow and sighed. "Come, they wish to toast our success before we part ways."

As the two clans gathered together around the laird, Brennus entered the circle to stand beside him.

"We've not yet defeated the *famhairean*, but I'll wager that willnae be long in coming now," Maddock said, winking at Brennus. "So, lift your bottles, lads, to the McAra and the Skaraven. Long may we remain steadfast friends."

"To our clans." Brennus touched his bottle to the laird's, and took a long drink as he thought of how simpler it would be if the nurse had never been taken. Then he realized the course to take.

Likely the lass is anxious to return to her time. I must send the McAra healer back.

Chapter Twenty-Three

⁂

HIDING FROM THE mortals had infuriated Murdina, until the earth had swallowed them whole and something seized her. She fought against the hard arms pressing her against the unyielding chest. Her nose and mouth filled with dirt as she tried to scream, convinced she had been bespelled back into the endless darkness of the Storr. Why hadn't Hendry saved her? Why hadn't he killed her, as he'd promised?

Hadn't Hendry promised to?

Slamming through a wall of rock, Murdina felt cold air pour over her as Dha dragged her from the pit in the earth. She threw her arms around him as she coughed out the soil, and sobbed until Hendry took her from him. He held her against his filthy robe.

"Why?" she shrieked into the grimy wool. "Why would you do this to me?"

"We had to escape, beauty mine," he told her. "If the McAra had taken us, then all of it would have been for naught."

"Wood Dream hurt?" Tri asked, hovering anxiously beside them.

"No, my friend. 'Tis only old fear and sorrow, and now 'tis over." Hendry drew back and used his thumbs to wipe away the tears from her face. "Dinnae you see? They shall never find us here, lover mine. They shall never even think to look."

Murdina blinked to clear her eyes, and saw the remains of the old ritual circle where she had been initiated as a novice.

"Oh, Hendry."

He took her arm, and walked with her through the barren forest, following the trail that led to the ruins of the Wood Dream settlement. The stone hearth of his cottage still stood at the very back, now almost buried in the plants that had grown wild from his spell garden.

Falling to her knees, Murdina pressed her mouth to the scarred soil and tasted the magic that had never been dispelled. To be returned here made memories pour through her battered mind. Here she had skipped as a girl, tiptoed after Hendry as a lass, and slipped through the darkness to meet him as his lover. They had buried their parents here, and loved in secret for so long.

It had been over a thousand years since she had dwelled here, and yet it felt as if she had left only yesterday. She looked up at him and smiled through the tears.

"You brought me home."

Chapter Twenty-Four

꧁🐝꧂

CADEYRN HELPED ALTHEA from the river outside Dun Mor. But when he made to accompany her on the path, she patted his arm.

"Go, Cade," she said. "I can find the stronghold."

"My lady," he said gratefully and took off at a run.

A powerful dread moved his feet but he refused to give up hope, as he dashed into Dun Mor's labyrinthine entry. Inside the great hall Rowan and Perrin sat swaddled in tartans by the hearth. Rowan's arm now lay in a sling, while her sister held one of Ruadri's herbal compresses to the back of her neck. Though they saw him, he couldn't stop to speak.

At the curtained entry to Ruadri's chamber he paused and pressed his hand against one of the raven carvings in the stone threshold.

"Please, let her be awake," he whispered.

He stopped a step inside when he saw Lily on the shaman's treatment table. He had wrapped her in blankets, and now stood over her head, his eyes closed as he murmured under his breath. A small pot of smoldering herbs laced the air with fragrant tendrils of smoke. Lily lay very still, with only the slight rise and fall of her chest to show she yet lived.

On the opposite end of the table Emeline hovered, leaning on a makeshift cane to keep her weight off her ankle. A length of linen was wrapped around her waist, and spots of blood stained it where it covered the spear wound to her side. She glared at Ruadri so intently she didn't seem to realize Cadeyrn had joined them.

He went to the table, unable to wait another moment to touch his lady. Her hand felt cool and so still in his. "How does she fare?"

The shaman opened his eyes to regard

him. "Naught has changed since you left the lady, Brother. She remains unaware and unable to move from the apoplexy. I've attempted a seeking spell to search out any thoughts she may have, but there arenae any. 'Tis a sign that her sleep may be one from which she cannae awake."

"Oh, bollocks," Emeline said, a hard edge to her voice. "I've seen many stroke patients recover and learn to speak and move again. The same with coma patients. There have been people who've woken up after decades of... Oh, never mind." She grimaced at Cadeyrn. "Lily needs only time to rest and heal, lad. When she's stronger, she'll wake."

"If she sleeps too long, her body shall wither," Ruadri countered. "To give the lady a chance of life we must find the means with which to wake her."

The nurse made a contemptuous sound. "With your mutterings and burning weeds?" She grimaced and pressed a hand to her wounded side.

"You need that tended to," Cadeyrn told her.

Emeline wiped the transfer of blood from

her palm to a rag. "The spear only pierced my abdominal oblique muscles. I'll be fine."

"Mistress McAra willnae permit me to treat her wounds," Ruadri said. He flicked a glance at her. "When I offered she claimed I'm naught but a Roman hag."

"Witch doctor," she corrected, "and who could blame me?" She gestured around them. "I wouldnae be surprised to find shrunken heads and voodoo dolls in this chamber of horrors. Look at that clutch of pots and vials. How can you call yourself a healer when you can't even properly label your concoctions?"

"I've only to sniff them to ken the mixture," Ruadri told her.

"Oh, so you practice medicine by *smell*. I should have guessed." The nurse shook her head. "He's no' putting a finger on me or my wounds. I'll treat myself." She glanced down at Lily, and the tight line of her mouth softened. "She will come back to us, Cade."

Ruadri watched her go before he pinched the bridge of his nose. "I thought she would be so different. Gentle and kind, like Lady Althea."

Cadeyrn hardly heard him as he stroked

Lily's small hand and stared down at her pale face. Carefully he slipped his arms beneath her still form and picked her up from the table.

"I'm taking her to my chambers."

"Cade, you shouldnae," the shaman said, but then sighed. "No, you should. You should spend every moment you may with her. When her breathing... If it slows, then you shall ken that her passing is upon her. Hold her close and speak gently to her. Let her ken that she goes with your love."

"She's no' dying," he told the shaman. "I'll drag her back from the afterlife if I must."

"But she may return," Ruadri said. "Druids may reincarnate, if they choose." He saw Cadeyrn's expression and ducked his head. "Forgive me, Brother. I but wish to give you some comfort."

"You sound like a tree-knower," Cadeyrn said, and immediately regretted the insult. "See to the others, and have Rowan attend to Emeline."

Carrying Lily through the Great Hall and down into the stronghold's lower levels, Cadeyrn felt only the light, soft weight of her against him. He'd always wondered why he'd never wanted a woman of his own, and now he knew. He'd been waiting for Lily. He'd been waiting for her to find him, even when he had not known that he was.

Inside his chambers, he took her to his bed and carefully lowered her onto the linens. He lit the oil lamps and left her to draw some warm water from the hall cistern. When he returned he placed a bowl of it beside the bed.

Tearing a sleeve from one of his old semats, Cadeyrn soaked it and began to wash the blood from her unmoving face. The faint whisper of her breath remained slow and shallow, and she did not stir. Once he had cleaned away the dark streaks he removed her damp clothing, and gently washed her body before he dressed her in his finest tunic.

She might never again wake, but she would always sleep beside him.

"I would see you in better than my garments, my lady," he told her as he picked her up and climbed onto the bed to hold her in his arms. "With your hair you should wear amber silks, and black velvets studded with golden beads. Skirts that flutter when you walk, and your hair loose upon your shoulders. You have such wondrous hair." He brushed a strand of it from her cheek. "When I dreamed of you, I so wished to touch it."

Cadeyrn talked to her more of the life he knew they would never have now. Of walking with her through the Great Wood, and taking her to the old watch blind. There she could sit with him in the darkness and watch the owls as they awoke and flew on their nocturnal hunts. He described the exhilaration of climbing up to the Great Plateau, and bracing the wind to look upon the beauty of the Red Hills spreading out for miles around them.

"When we'd come home at night, lass, I'd bring you here to strip you bare, and wrap you in long strands of dark pearls to mark where I should kiss you." Cadeyrn shifted his hand to her chin and traced the sweet curves of her lips. "I'd map every inch of your skin with my mouth, and then start anew, over and again."

But no matter the words he spoke or the gentle touches he gave, his lady did not stir. Gently he placed his hand over her heart, remembering how she had opened his. Bitterness as he'd never known choked off more words. Though he was changed by her—and for her—the cruel neglect of the Gods would now take her from him. Even his battle spirit had played its part, binding her to him in body and soul. Immortality suddenly stretched before him, as dark and cold as his thoughts.

A faint glitter drew his gaze to his hand on her chest. His black raven clan ring glinted in the lamplight. He frowned at the memory of Brennus using his, still bespelled with the magic that had awakened the Skaraven, to bring back Althea from death. Seeing her healed and made immortal had so stunned Cadeyrn that he'd dropped like a stone. Though his lady was not dead, only locked in an endless slumber, Cadeyrn's heartbeat quickened.

Might the ring rescue her?

He rubbed his thumb over the raven carving, the blackened wood made as hard as stone by time. In his heart he knew she would never awaken again on her own. Nor did he know how to use the magic that might yet be trapped in his ring to heal her. The spell contained in the ring awoke the dead.

She'd willingly paid the price to save him

and the other ladies. If the Gods reckoned the weight and balance of mortal lives, surely that mattered. Cadeyrn removed his ring, and pulled the leather lacing from his tunic.

"'Tis how Brennus gave his to Althea," he told her as he slid the ring onto the lacing, and then tied it around her neck. "Mayhap if you go from me, 'twill bring you back."

Lily didn't move, and no great flash of light came from the ring. Rising from the bed, Cadeyrn covered her with the linens and sat on the edge to hold his head in his hands. Then he went down on his knees beside it and pressed his hands to the stone floor. He wanted to dash his head against it until his skull split. He wanted to soak it with tears. But instead he gave voice to all that was in his heart.

"Please," he murmured as he touched his brow to the stone, humbling himself completely. "You brought her to me. You mated her to me. I failed her, I ken that, but so did you. Guide me and I shall do anything you ask. Anything to save her."

Still there was nothing. Cadeyrn knew what he was asking: the impossible. As long as she wore his ring there might be some hope if she died, but as long as she lived she remained lost to him.

A terrible thought arose in his mind. If she died while she wore his ring...

"No," he yelled, his fists pounding the floor. Fury surged through him as he shot to his feet. "Lily fought bravely for us, without a care of what 'twould do to her. I would give anything, even my own life, to save hers. But I willnae take what little you have left her. Do you hear me? I love her and *I willnae kill her.*"

All around the room his possessions began to rattle, and the sound of something huge and furious filled the chamber. Cadeyrn threw himself over Lily as a sweeping wave of magic blasted out from the bed, smashing everything in its path. The bed collapsed in a heap, as splinters of wood rained down to pelt his back and head.

Gods, what had he done?

A soft, muffled sound made him stop breathing.

Pushing himself up on his hands, Cadeyrn looked down at his love's pale face, that now went rosy with new color. Her long hair flowed out over his hands and arms until a great mass of it rippled across the bed.

He blinked, convinced now that he was dreaming. "Lily?"

Her eyes slowly opened, and she looked at him as if puzzled. "Cade." She slid a glance to one side of them and then the other. "Is this Dun Mor?" When he nodded, she frowned. "You chaps need a housekeeper. I only cook, you know. My father always had servants for the rest."

Cadeyrn kissed her, laughed, and kissed her again. The taste of her lips made him feel drunk, and the soft sounds she made against his mouth rammed desire through him until his cock felt as if it might burst.

"Where are you going?" she demanded after he pulled away and vaulted from the bed. She sat up and watched him as he began barricading the door. "Or not going, then?"

Outside in the passage, the thuds of running boots drew close, and someone hammered on the door and shouted in a deep voice for Cadeyrn.

"We're fine, and my lady's awake," he called back. "Leave us alone for the day. And the night. Fack no, we'll come out when we want food."

Lily climbed off the bed and was holding out the much-longer tresses of her hair. "Good God. What's happened to me?"

Cadeyrn took her hands in his and told her everything that had happened since he'd taken her and their ladies from the pool at the falls. He told her of Coig's end, and what that had revealed. Finally, he spoke of the apoplexy that had put her into an endless sleep, and how he'd refused to kill her even when he thought it might awaken her to immortality.

"So, you told the Gods to sod off when it came to killing me," she said once he'd finished. "Yet you knew I wouldn't come out of the coma."

"I couldnae take your life from you." He drew her down on the mattress beside him. "So much of it has been stolen from you by your father, and the mad druids, and Coig. How could I take what little you might have left?"

She thought for a moment. "Maybe they brought me back because this time *you* made the sacrifice."

"I dinnae care why you awakened, only that you have." He kissed her brow. "You've been made immortal by it as I was. We'll no' grow old together, Lily, because we'll never grow old. But if you'll have me, we'll be together always."

She laced her fingers through his. "I think I've got you already, boyo. Since I love you madly, that's settled." She glanced over her shoulder at the splinters of wood covering most of the blanket. "But we need a new bed, I think. I don't fancy shagging on a stone floor."

Chapter Twenty-Five

R UADRI KEPT TO the shadows as he came out of his chamber and into the great hall. Althea sat speaking softly with the healer. The sisters had gone, likely to bed. For a moment he simply watched Emeline, and the way the firelight etched shadows on her pale face. She had eyes like jewels, and hair as fine and dark as jet, and a tongue like a skinning blade.

Since she could not see him Ruadri allowed his gaze to wander. Beside Althea's tall, willowy form the nurse looked lush and exotic, like a goddess from another land. He could see her McAra blood in her coloring, and the stubborn set of her jaw, but there was so much more to admire and yearn to touch.

No' that I'll ever put a finger on her, the shaman reminded himself.

Without warning Brennus arrived, and Althea hurried over to greet her husband. She ushered him and the others over to the hearth to warm themselves, and called for Kelturan to bring hot brews. No one but Ruadri noticed Emeline hobbling away.

Following her made him feel foolish, but he told himself that she knew nothing of the stronghold and might become lost. She limped all the way back to Kanyth's forge, where she stood studying the large table covered with tools and stacks of iron bars.

"I can feel you there," Emeline said without turning around to face him.

Moving cautiously, Ruadri joined her. "I didnae mean to frighten you."

"I'm no' afraid." She regarded him. "What do you want?"

Being this close to her made him feel as if he were basking in a spring sun. "To ken why you've taken such a dislike to me."

"I dinnae dislike you," Emeline said, smiling a little. "I've been rude to you, and I'm sorry for that."

Here now she was as he had dreamt her, a lovely, kind lady who had been stolen from her home. He knew her to be hurt and frightened, and yet she pretended the opposite. She had suffered greatly, but she would not show it to him.

"I want only to help with your wound." He nodded at her side. "'Twill need cleaning and bandaging. I should see to your foot, and mayhap your jaw."

"I've bruised the jaw, broken the ankle, and the side wound still bleeds." All the emotion left her face. "But I ken what you truly want, Ruadri Skaraven, and you cannae have that."

He frowned. "What do you believe I want, my lady?"

"Me." She turned and hobbled off.

Chapter Twenty-Six

IN THE FRONT room at the Aviemore inn, Oriana sat watching for the skinny lad who delivered scrolls from the town's dovecote. Since releasing the Skaraven shaman from his duty as Watcher, the messages between Bhaltair Flen and Ruadri had abruptly stopped, only to begin again in a flurry, some arriving every two hours.

"Here you be, young mistress," the innkeeper's wife said as she came into the room with a tray and placed it on the table beside her. As she straightened she swayed a little. "Do me a kindness again and take this meal up to your master. My knees arenae wanting to traipse up the stairs today."

Oriana looked up at Mistress Moray's broad face, and saw the thick veins distended in her forehead. She could almost hear the rapid pounding of her pulse, and noted the faint bluish color around her lips. She knew that the mortal's stout body, poor diet and lifetime of hard work had worn out her heart. She would not survive another year.

In another time Oriana might have even cared. Now it just provided her with some mild amusement. What would the mortal do if she knew she had such little time left? Would she cry and beg, and waste precious days mourning all that she would never do?

Not that she would ever do more than cater to strangers for a few coins.

"Master Flen sleeps now, my lady," Oriana said. She always made sure to call her that, as it pleased her. Keeping beguiled those who served her purpose had required much of the same simpering and flattering. "But I shall carry it up and leave it by his bedside."

"My thanks," Mistress Moray said and gave her a tired smile. "I've yours in the kitchen when you want it."

Oriana tarried for another few minutes, and then stood as she saw the rail-thin lad hurrying to the inn's door. She met him there, bobbing impatiently to his clumsy bow, and held out her hand.

"No, I cannae, Mistress," the lad said.

"But you must. My master has gone abed," she told the messenger. "I shall hold the scroll for him."

"There's two this time." The lad dug in his pocket for them, and then held them out of her reach. "My da said I shouldnae give them to you again. They arenae meant for your eyes. He said that I should put them in Master Flen's hands."

"Shall I tell your da what you made me do behind the milkshed?" Oriana smiled at his confused expression. "Och, you dinnae recall it? 'Twas very bad. He'll whip you for putting hands on so young a lass as me."

His eyes widened. "I never did the like."

"Oh, aye, but I'll make him believe it. Such shocking things." Before he could move, she reached out and dug her nails into the back of his hand, dragging them down. "And

I'll tell him I scratched you while you held me down." She showed him the blood under her nails. "Now give me the facking scrolls."

Going white, he thrust them in her hands and fled the inn.

Oriana carried the scrolls into the front room, where she sat and sipped some of the brew intended for her master as she deciphered the coded messages. The first stated that the druidesses taken from the future had been rescued and moved to Dun Mor. That infuriated Oriana, as she had hoped to use one or more of the females once they had been delivered to the druids.

The second message invited Bhaltair Flen to the McAra stronghold to consult with the laird and the Skaraven Chieftain on an urgent matter concerning the *famhairean*.

Tugging on a piece of her hair, Oriana read the message a second time. Brennus despised Bhaltair, and had made it plain that he would not permit him near his clan or their stronghold. Now he bid him to attend him as a guest of the McAra. In one sense the invitation completely ruined her plans, but in another it offered a simpler alternative.

Oriana looked at the circlet of hair she had pulled out of her scalp, neatly wound around her purpled fingertip. A vague throbbing at her temple told her she'd pulled too hard again. She tugged off the hair ring, tossing it into the fire to watch it burn.

Gwyn had caught her in the act once, and warned her to cease the habit before she plucked herself bald. That had been the day she'd so wanted to tell him the truth, and show him what she had hidden from him for so long. At the time her body had not yet fully matured, however, and she could not tell him until she stood as his equal in form as well as heart. She knew once she revealed the truth that he would no longer be able to hide his desires.

Two years shy of her maturity, Gwyn had been murdered.

It had nearly gutted her to see what the *famhairean* had done to him, but Oriana had to see. She memorized every wound, every indignity. She'd gone back to their cottage, and crawled into Gwyn's bed, and buried her face in the hollow his head had left in the pillow. As the madness came over her she'd screamed into it and wept upon it. By dawn when the headman came to see her, it had become soaked through with her tears.

Rising from that bed had taken all of her strength, but by then she had come to know what she had to do. She spoke to the headman like the girl he thought her to be, and begged to be permitted to take the news to Gwyn's old friend, Bhaltair.

Oriana carefully rewound the scrolls, adding them to the meal tray before she took it upstairs to the room she shared with the old druid.

Bhaltair lay on one of the narrow beds, his face slack and his breathing deep and regular. Oriana had known better than to dose his drinks, as he remained paranoid about how they tasted since being poisoned by a renegade druid. Instead she put her sleeping potion in his evening meal. Since she prepared most of his food, or carried it up from the inn's kitchen, she could assure he slept soundly every night, allowing her to slip away and do as she wished.

She did much that would have shocked the

old druid. She'd used the groves to search every place she thought Dun Mor might be, to no avail. She'd stolen coin from rich mortals to give to those who had seen the Skaraven, although none of them offered anything but wild tales of battling warriors who vanished into lochs and rivers. She'd even eavesdropped on the McAra laird while he bedded his wife, but the man only spoke of his proud cock and his love for his lady, two things that bored Oriana so much she'd nearly dozed off.

As if he knew her thoughts Bhaltair muttered in his sleep.

Oriana set the tray aside, and took the long ritual dagger from the false bottom in her satchel. She had honed the double-edged blade herself, murmuring under her breath as she worked it against the whetstone. It gleamed in the firelight, cold and razor-sharp, and when she stood over the old druid's bed she could see herself choosing a vein to slice open. His pudgy neck had several and, if she cut deeply enough, she'd make him choke on his own blood.

You who might have saved him. You selfish bastart.

Bhaltair Flen would die by her hand. She had absolutely no doubt of it. When she ended him, he would be wide awake and gazing up at her. He would see the dripping dagger in her hand, and she would tell him why. He would know how richly he deserved his murder before he went into the well of stars. There he would stay in shame for what he had done to her and Gwyn.

If he didn't care to remain there, and returned in another form, she would simply kill him again, and again, and again. She would end Bhaltair Flen in every one of his lives, until he understood that she would never again allow him to dwell in the mortal realm.

At that moment Oriana's fury nearly drove her blade into his neck. Then she remembered the second message, and the rare opportunity it presented.

"Sleep well, old fool," she whispered as she turned her back on him. "You may deny me my vengeance today, but soon I shall have it of you and the Skaraven. Very soon."

THE END

• • • • •

Another Immortal Highlander awaits you in Ruadri (Immortal Highlander, Clan Skaraven Book 3).

For a sneak peek, turn the page.

Sneak Peek

Ruadri (Immortal Highlander, Clan Skaraven Book 3)

Excerpt

CHAPTER ONE

STANDING ALONE IN the medieval high-
land forest, Emeline McAra didn't see snow
drifts. Somehow winter had transformed the
world into a bridal boutique stuffed with
wedding dresses. Dozens of them surrounded
her, all big, beautiful confections of white satin
and lace waiting to be donned and admired.
Ice and frost became ruffled hems, beaded
trains, and crystal-sequined headpieces.
Beyond the gowns the river had frozen into an

ivory carpet of sparkling light, down which wand-thin beauties might solemnly saunter as they modeled the latest gown trends: off-the-shoulder bodices, plunging V-necks, side cutouts, and statement sleeves.

Winter, Emeline decided, hated her.

"Healer McAra?"

Emeline might ignore the dark beauty of Shaman Ruadri Skaraven's impossibly deep voice, but she couldn't escape his presence—or the emotions he brought with him. Even before Emeline became a nurse she could sense other people's feelings, probably from the years she'd spent caring for her taciturn elderly parents. Since being taken with four other women to fourteenth-century Scotland, the dial on her gift had been turned up to full blast.

Time traveling had turned Emeline's natural, gentle empathy into a nightmare.

Since she'd arrived in the Middle Ages, the emotions of others came to her in a synesthetic jumble of colors, textures, sounds and scents. Depending on who projected the feelings, their anger could be a bright red hammer pounding inside her head, or an icy black torrent drenching her skin. Another person's worry enveloped her in a too-small straitjacket of stifling, damp wool. Fear tasted metallic and sharp, like licking a honed knife, while pain smelled of the aftermath of such a foolish act: tears and blood.

During Emeline's first week as a prisoner of the mad druids and their bizarre inhuman guards, the bombardment had never let up. Every time one of the other four women panicked, Emeline had been jolted and pummeled and smothered by their terror. Their situation had grown so desperate that the cacophony of fear from the others had made her constantly retch. She'd only just learned how to block the worst of the sensory attacks to protect herself, but she first had to be prepared for them.

Emeline had never been ready for anything about this man. To look at him wrenched at her heart, just as it had the very first moment he'd walked out of the shadows last night.

"Do you want for something?" Ruadri asked from behind her.

That question almost made her laugh out

loud. How she wanted for something—so many things. To be held, comforted, and loved. To know if she would survive this insanity. To discover what it was like to be kissed. To tell him that she had never believed in love at first sight.

To punch the shaman square in the nose for making her a believer.

"No, thank you," she said.

The words hurt her tight throat as she built the blockade in her mind to keep out his emotions, while keeping a tight grip on her own.

Emeline had no intention of making a ninny of herself, so she went back to her memory of the bridal shop in Inverness. All the magnificent, snowy gowns there had resembled an army of delicate, unsullied confection. They seemed silently smug, too, as if they knew she'd never have a reason to wear any of them. The mist around her combined with the pale sunlight glittering on the tree branches to become veils adorned with crystals and silk flowers, also forever out of her reach. The air in the shop had smelled of roses, but here every breath felt so cold and clean, so pure. Almost too beautiful for her to breathe.

"But why can't you try on the bloody dress?" Meribeth Campbell demanded from her memory of that last day in the twenty-first century. As always, her gleaming blonde curls had lovingly framed Meri's pretty face, even when it went rosy with temper. "The blue is perfect for you. I even got the high neckline you fancied. Really, Em, there's nothing wrong with it. You'll look lovely."

"I ordered a size eighteen, Meri," Emeline said, eyeing the sapphire bridesmaid's dress brought in for her fitting. Judging by the dimensions, she might be able to squeeze one leg or arm into it, if she first starved for another month and then buttered herself. "I think they missed a digit."

The shop clerk checked the tag and grimaced. "It *is* a size eight, Miss."

"Of course, it is," Meribeth said, throwing her hands in the air. "How long until you can get the right size?" She scowled as the clerk went to consult with the seamstress who was waiting to do any needed alterations. "I can't believe this. My bloody wedding is next week."

This might be her last chance to get out of making a spectacle of herself, Emeline thought.

"You have four other bridesmaids, Meri. You'll not need me."

"What I need is... Oh, damn, I know what happened." She retrieved her mobile and pressed some buttons. "Lauren, it's me. Did Bride's Blush deliver your gown? What size is it? Och, the wallapers. No, don't send it back, it's Emmy's. She's yours here." She dropped her voice to a fierce whisper. "No, she hasn't tried it on, you goose. How could she?"

Meri didn't have to say it was half Emeline's size. Everyone knew how fat she was. Especially their coworker Lauren Reid, who dropped sly digs about her weight when-ever she could. Ironically Emeline had been on a strict diet for the last eight weeks in order to slim down enough to get into an off-the-rack dress. No one had noticed, not even Meri. Still, as her best friend and worst enemy nattered on, Emeline kept her forced smile firmly riveted in place. So what if she was black affronted by two reed-thin women who'd never know what deliberate starvation felt like? She had to stop making this about her. It was all for Meri.

"Healer McAra," Ruadri said as he came closer, the snow crunching under his boots. "Havenae you yet slept?"

Tears burned in Emeline's eyes as she was yanked back to the present—or the past—or whenever she was.

"I'm no' tired."

And now she was lying. She'd tried to sleep, but the pain of her side wound and ankle combined with thoughts of him had made it impossible. She should tell him that since coming here last night she'd never felt more hurt, exhausted, or anxious.

The last was *his* fault. Since the first moment she'd seen the shaman he'd made her as nervous as a drunkard in a minefield.

"'Tis cold," Ruadri said as he stopped just behind her. His scent rolled over her. He smelled of something darkly decadent and spicy, like a chocolate spiked with serrano. "You should come inside, out of the wind."

Come inside with you, and find a dark room, and throw myself at you, yes. Oh, please, yes. The chill seeping through the wool cloak Emeline wore suddenly felt biting, or was it his worry, growing sharper? *He doesnae care about me. I'm just a great bausy nuisance.*

"I'm no' a bairn."

"Aye, that I ken." Ruadri came to stand beside her and held out his huge black and amber plaid tartan. "You're shivering. Wrap yourself in this."

He was too close now, and any moment he would touch her with those large, strong hands that looked so capable and clever. Emeline didn't think she could stand that, and then felt the sensory wall inside her head begin to crumble.

"No, thank you."

Blast her ankle, she had to get away from him this instant. Emeline limped away, stopping at the edge of the river to pull back her hood and look down at the blurry reflection of herself in the ice, made only more vivid by the sunrise. For weeks she'd been a battered, starved prisoner, and it showed. So many snarls tangled her black hair it resembled a mass of poorly-done dreadlocks. The yellowish-brown bruises on the puffy side of her face made it look like a moldy cheese wheel. Her mouth seemed like a smear of faded red paint beneath the sunken hollows of her eyes.

Death oan a pirn stick, her grandmother would have said.

A shadow stretched over her reflection like the wings of some fallen angel. "If you keep walking in that splint you may shatter that ankle, Healer."

Before she could stop herself, Emeline turned to face the shaman's broad chest. Well over two meters tall, and as wide as two caber tossers, Ruadri completely dwarfed her. She wondered if she simply talked to that wall of muscle that this time she might maintain her composure. But no, she couldn't see the shaman and not look up into his striking face, or his enigmatic gray eyes, the color of moon shadows. Silver spilled from his temples into his hair in two wide swaths, chasing the blue-violet glints that dawn had painted on some of the black strands.

Handsome men made Emeline nervous. Ruadri stunned and terrified her.

"I'm no' cold. My ankle's mending. I've told you I'll look after myself." She realized her voice had risen almost to a shout, and quickly dragged in a steadying breath. "I've been through an ordeal, Shaman. All I wish is to be left alone."

"I cannae do that," Ruadri said. "Ever."

• • • • •

Buy *Ruadri (Immortal Highlander, Clan Skaraven Book 3)*

DO ME A FAVOR?

You can make a big difference.

Reviews are the most powerful tools I have when it comes to getting attention for my books. Much as I'd like it, I don't have the financial muscle of a New York publisher. I can't take out full page ads in the newspaper—not yet, anyway.

But I do have something much more powerful. It's something that those publishers would kill for: **a committed and loyal group of readers.**

Honest reviews of my books help bring them to the attention of other readers. If you've enjoyed this book I would so appreciate it if you could spend a few minutes leaving a review—any length you like.

Thank you so much!

MORE BOOKS BY HH

For a complete, up-to-date book list, visit
HazelHunter.com/books.

Get notifications of new releases and special
promotions by joining my newsletter!

Glossary

Here are some brief definitions to help you navigate the medieval world of the Immortal Highlanders.

acolyte - novice druid in training
Am Monadh Ruadh - the original Scots Gaelic name for the Cairngorm mountains, which translates to English as "the red hills"
apoplexy, apoplectic - medieval terms for "stroke" and "suffering from a stroke"
arse - British slang for "ass"
aye - yes
bairn - child
bastart - bastard
baws - balls, testicles

beastly - British slang for something horrible or arduous

Beinn Nibheis – old Scots Gaelic for Ben Nevis, the highest mountain in Scotland

besotted - British slang for strongly infatuated

blaeberry - European fruit that resembles the American blueberry

bleeding - British obscenity, roughly equivalent to "damned" but much more offensive in the UK

bloke - British slang for a male

blethering - chatting

bleezin' -drunk

blind - cover device

blood kin - genetic relatives

bloody - British obscenity, see bleeding

boon - gift or favor

boyo - British slang for a boy or man

Bràithrean an fhithich - Brethren of the raven

braw - Scottish slang for "outstanding"

brieve - a writ

brilliant - British slang for excellent or marvelous

buckler - shield

bugger - British slang for a contemptible person

cac - Scots gaelic for "shit"

caibeal - Scots Gaelic for "chapel"

cairn - a pile or stack of stones

Caledonia - ancient Scotland

cannae - can't

caraidean - Scots Gaelic for "friends"

chap - British slang for a male

cheeky - British slang for slightly disrespectful

Chieftain - the head of a specific Pritani tribe

chundering - British slang for throwing up

clodhoppers - British slang for work boots

clout - strike

cocked up - British slang for something done very badly

coddle - pamper

codswallop - British slang for "nonsense"

comely - attractive

conclave - druid ruling body

conclavist - member of the druid ruling body

cosh - British slang for "hit"

couldnae - couldn't

cow - derogatory term for woman

croft - small rented farm

cross - British slang for "angry"

cudgel - wooden club

daft - crazy

demi - French term for a half-size bottle of champagne; holds 375 ml

dinnae - don't

disincarnate - commit suicide

doesnae - doesn't

dru-wid - Proto Celtic word; an early form of "druid"

eagalsloc - synonym for "oubliette"; coined from Scots Gaelic for "fear" and "pit"; an inescapable hole or cell where prisoners are left to die

ducat - a gold European trade coin

ell - ancient unit of length measurement, equal to approximately 18 inches

epicure - a person who takes particular interest and/or pleasure in gourmet dining and drinking

fack - fuck

facking - fucking

famhair - Scots Gaelic for giant (plural, famhairean)

fathom - understand

feart - Scottish or Irish for afraid

firesteel - a piece of metal used with flint to create sparks for fire-making fortlet - a little fort

fortnight - British slang for a two-week period of time

Francia - France

Francian - French

Gaul - ancient region that included France, Belgium, southern Netherlands, southwestern Germany, and northern Italy

Germania - Germany

goosed - Scottish slang for "smashed"

gormless - British slang for someone with an acute lack of common sense

granary - a storehouse for threshed grain

greyling - species of freshwater fish in the salmon family

hasnae - hasn't

Hispania - Roman name for the Iberian peninsula (modern day Portugal and Spain)

incarnation - one of the many lifetimes of a druid

isnae - isn't

jolly good - British slang for "excellent"

keeker - black eye

ken - know

kip - British slang for "nap"

knackered - British slang for exhausted

lad - boy

laird - lord

land of the white bear - the Arctic

larder - pantry

lass - girl

league - distance measure of approximately three miles

leannan - Scots Gaelic for "beloved"

lochan - a small lakelot - British slang for a group, usually made up of people

magic folk - druids

make a hash of it - British slang, to do something badly

manky - British slang for "disgusting"

mate (nickname) - British slang for "friend"

mayhap - maybe

mind-move - telekinesis

minging - stinky

mojo - American slang for "magic"

morion - a brown or black variety of quartz

mustnae - must not

naught - nothing

no' - not

nod off - British slang for going to sleep

NOSAS - North of Scotland Archaeology Society

nutjob - American slang for a crazy or foolish person

nutter - British slang for a mentally-disturbed person

on about - British slang for "talking about"

on the mooch - Scottish slang for spying on someone á la a Peeping Tom

oubliette - a dungeon with an opening only at the top

ovate - Celtic priest or natural philosopher

pike - pole

plonker - British slang for "idiot"

prattling - to talk for a long time on inconsequential matters

Pritani - Britons (one of the people of southern Britain before or during Roman times)

quim - medieval slang for the female genitals

quisling - a traitor who collaborates with the enemy

reeks like an alky's carpet - very smelly

ruddy - a British intensifier and euphemism for bloody

scarper - British slang for "run away"

schiltron - a medieval battle formation used to form a living barrier or wall of troops

scullery - a small back room off the kitchen where the dishes or laundry are washed

scunner - Scottish slang for an object or person that causes dislike and/or nausea

shag - British slang for sexual intercourse

shambles - British slang for an extensive or serious mess

shambolic - British slang for "chaotic"

shite - British slang for "shit"

shouldnae - shouldn't

side ladders - the slatted upper sides on the back of a medieval cart or wagon

skelp - strike, slap, or smack

slee - sly, cunning

sod (verb) - British slang for "screw"

sod all - British slang for "nothing"

solar - rooms in a medieval castle that served as the family's private living and sleeping quarters

solicitor - British term for lawyer

speak-seer - a druid who can communicate with the dead and channel their voices

spew - vomit

staunch weed - yarrow

stone (weight) - British weight measurement equal to 14 lbs.

Tha mi a 'gealltainn - Scots Gaelic for "I promise"

'tis - it is

'tisnt - it isn't

tor - large, freestanding rock outcrop

tree-knower - the Skaraven nickname for the druids of their time

thick with - closely involved, relating to "thick as thieves"

transom - a weight-bearing support crossbar

trencher - wooden platter for food

trews - trousers

'twas - it was

'twere - it was

'twill - it will

'twould - it would

uisge beatha - old Scots Gaelic for "whiskey"

undercroft - a room in a lower level of a castle used for storage

vole - small rodent related to the mouse

wanker - British slang for a useless person

wasnae - wasn't

watchlight - a term for a grease-soaked rush stalk, used as a candle in medieval times wazzock - British slang for "idiot"

wee - small

wench - girl or young woman

willnae - will not

wouldnae - would not

Yank - UK slang for "American"

Pronunciation Guide

A selection of the more challenging words in the Immortal Highlander, Clan Skaraven series.

Ailpin - ALE-pin
Althea Jarden - al-THEE-ah JAR-den
Am Monadh Ruadh - im monih ROOig
Aon - OOH-wen
apoplexy - APP-ah-plecks-ee
Aviemore - AH-vee-more
Beinn Nibheis - ben NIH-vis
Bhaltair Flen - BAHL-ter Flen
Black Cuillin - COO-lin
Bràithrean an fhithich - BRAH-ren ahn EE-och
Brennus Skaraven - BREN-ess skah-RAY-ven

Bridei - BREE-dye

caibeal - KYB-al

cac - kak

Caderyn - KAY-den

cairn - KAYRN

Cailean Lusk - KAH-len Luhsk

caraidean - KAH-rah-deen

Coig - COH-egg

Dha - GAH

Domnall - DON-uhl

eagalsloc - EHK-al-slakh

Emeline McAra - EM-mah-leen mac-CAR-ah

famhair - FAV-ihr

Ferath - FAIR-ahth

Galan - gal-AHN

Gwyn Embry - gah-WIN AHM-bree

Hendry Greum - HEN-dree GREE-um

Kanyth - CAN-ith

Kelturan - KEL-tran

Liath - LEE-ehth

Lily Stover - LILL-ee STOW-ver

lochan - LOHK-an

Maddock McAra - MAH-duck mac-CAR-ah

Manath - MAN-ahth

McFarlan - mick-FAR-len

Moray - MORE-ray

Murdina Stroud - mer-DEE-nah STROWD

Ochd - OHK

Oriana Embry - or-ree-ANN-ah AHM-bree

Perrin Thomas - PEAR-in TOM-us

Rowan Thomas - ROW-en TOM-us

Ruadri - roo-ah-DREE

schiltron - SKILL-trahn

Taran - ter-RAN

Tha mi a 'gealltainn - HA mee a GYALL-ting

Tri - TREE

uisge beatha - OOSH-ka bah

Dedication

For Mr. H.

Copyright

Made in the USA
Columbia, SC
11 June 2018